FIVE lives... only ONE ending

DYING in
BRIGHTON

from the BESTSELLING author

of 'Blonde BOY, Red LIPSTICK'

GEOFF BUNN

Nicola's story

The sky was overcast, threatening rain. All around people stood, most of them wearing black, some in other but equally sombre colours. There were white shirts and blouses under dark jackets and lightweight woollen coats. Polished shoes. Flowers, too. But these were not happy flowers.

A long row of shiny cars on the road, also black, polished even brighter than all the shoes, a thin grass verge between them and the pavement. Privet hedges between that pavement and the front gardens of the little terraced homes.

People were waiting, some of them dabbing at their cheeks with handkerchiefs.

The largest of the cars contained a wooden box with brass handles. Probably not solid brass, and the wood was almost certainly not oak. The box itself barely visible through a wall of garlands. Words like 'Mum' and 'Darling' could be read quite clearly.

Two young girls, sisters but very different, stood statue-like just a few feet away from the car with the wooden box. Both of them were very pretty, with huge dark eyes and almost jet hair. But it was the older of the two, aged about 9 years old, who was the prettier. She was also the one who looked the more worried, the more concerned.

Of course there was a deep and horrible – but quite natural – sadness within both of them. And that was clear on both of their faces, evident in their body posture, their hushed voices. Their mother was in that coffin.

But there was also, unmistakably, a look of worry on Nicola's face, the older girl. And every now and then, she lifted her head, ever so slightly, to look towards the half-hidden front door of her home. It was there, almost concealed behind the high privet hedge, and it was open. Still open. Still. It had been open for a long time. With people coming and going. Flowers. Other things. But by now, it really ought to have been firmly closed. Their father, Nicola and Jackie's father, ought to have been out here. The cars now moving. The funeral begun.

Instead of that, things were running late. And slowly, an unwanted tension arose.

Funerals were not a place for tension. Things were supposed to move inexorably towards their conclusion. That was part of the ritual. Sadness, grief and even, sometimes, small amounts of laughter were appropriate. But tension was not.

Suddenly there was movement at that front door. That half ajar door. Figures appeared. There was a loud slamming noise – something else out of place at a funeral – and three men, also wearing black, walked down the path and stood on the grass verge.

One of those, the tallest of them, was the girls' father.

Without thought or care, he took two long strides to where Nicola and Jackie stood, almost motionless, and then spoke with a venom he did not really feel. Directly at Nicola, into her large, dark and moist eyes, he said "You stupid girl. Don't ever bloody do that again. You'd drive anyone to despair. It's your fault your mother's dead!"

It was not Nicola's fault that her mother was dead.

Her father did not mean those words.

And no sooner had he said them than he wished he had not.

But life doesn't easily or readily undo such moments. And later, after the service, by the time he apologised for being so cross, told Nicola he hadn't meant it and then held his precious daughters close, it was already much too late. That moment – that awkward horrible clumsy moment – was now a part of their world.

In some hidden corner of her being, Nicola now believed that her mother had died because of her. *Because of her.*

It was bedtime, a week after the funeral, and the two girls were getting undressed.

"I don't want to go to school tomorrow", said Jackie.

"Why not?" asked Nicola, getting into bed and pulling the covers up as quickly as she could.

It was a very cold night and this was not a house with central heating.

"Mary Jones said she's going to beat me up".

Nicola's eyes opened-wide. "Why?"

Jackie shrugged. Sniffed. She was crying. She was only 18 months younger than Nicola but she was quite a bit smaller. And more fragile. Always catching colds. She had missed school for some months, once, because of measles and then, almost immediately afterwards, she had caught chicken pox.

Of course there was much more to Jackie's sadness than just some stupid threat made by a girl at school.

The reality of their loss, the emptiness, the loneliness – all of that – was only just now beginning to sink in. And even then they were both too young to really see or understand the enormity of it.

Sometimes – not very often, but sometimes – it would be the worst thing to lose a father. But much more often, whether boys or girls, and especially at such a crucial age, a child losing a mother was the very worst thing that could happen. The cruellest turn of fate.

Jackie climbed into bed.

Nicola looked at her little sister for a moment. "I'll be there", she said. "Don't be scared. If Mary whatever-her-name-is tries anything, she'll have to come through me first".

That was true. Nicola always looked out for her sister. She'd always done that. But she had done it even more since their mother had fallen ill, since the cancer had begun to kill her. Not because Nicola really understood what the cancer was. Not that she consciously took over her mother's role. But she did it anyway.

"Promise?" asked Jackie, still crying.

Nicola nodded, crossing herself.

Jackie sniffed and lay down, sobbing once or twice. Then she lay quiet. Still and quiet in the dark.

"Are you OK?" asked Nicola.

"No", came the quiet, petulant reply.

"What's wrong?" asked Nicola.

"I want my mom", Jackie cried. "I want my mom. I want mom back".

Nicola didn't hesitate. Freezing cold night or not, she climbed out of bed and got straight in with her sister. She put her arm around the smaller girl and pulled her in close.

And the two young girls fell asleep like that.

The following day, Nicola got herself and Jackie ready for school. It wasn't too difficult. Theirs was a school without uniforms. So a coat and a few clean clothes, already put out by their father, was almost all that was needed.

Nicola made sure that Jackie ate cereal and toast. Even though the younger girl wanted neither thing.

And then, as they walked out of the red door, and saw the rain falling, Nicola made sure that Jackie's coat was buttoned and that her hood was up too.

And so the two girls went to school.

They would not be back until around 4 pm. Their father had to work from 6 am to 2 pm and there would be no one at home to feed them. So lunch had been taken at school for some time now, ever since their mother had fallen ill. That was OK. School lunches weren't so bad. And it also meant that Nicola could keep an eye on Mary Jones.

And that was what she did.

Despite playing with her own friends, she kept a constant eye on Jackie and her group. And when Mary Jones did seem to get a bit too loud and bullying, Nicola quickly sorted her out.

"Our mom has just died", she told Mary. "Don't you think it would be better to leave Jackie alone at a time like this? How do you think you would feel?"

No aggression, no violence – just good, strong, calm and thoughtful words. It was an incredibly grown-up way to behave. And it worked too. Mary Jones apologised to Nicola and to Jackie and even began to play nicely with the younger sister.

Problem resolved.

Unfortunately when they got back home, trouble was waiting.

"Nicola", said father. "What have I told you about going out and making sure the front door is shut?"

Nicola didn't really know what her father was talking about.

"You went out to school and left the bloody door open", he said. "I came home this afternoon and found it open. Anyone could have walked in!"

Nicola hadn't given the door a thought. Because of the rain, she had been too busy buttoning up her sister's coat. But she couldn't remember shutting the door. Or not shutting it. And so she had no excuse, apparently, for going out and leaving that red door ajar.

And she knew that was a bad thing to do.

She felt stupid. Wrong.

Then her Dad said something else, she didn't really hear what, but she'd just had enough. So she shouted at him, told him to shut up.

"Don't you dare shout at me!" snapped her Dad.

And a pointless, irrational argument began.

And for the thousandth time, Nicola found herself in the wrong, in the eyes of her father. A father who had, after all, just watched his wife and partner die.

"Leave me alone!" she shouted. "You're always picking on me".

And with that, Nicola stormed off to bed, slamming all the doors she could.

The following day, which was a Saturday, she took a pair of scissors to her Dad's best suit.

Of course that was a stupid thing to do. And Nicola knew it even as she did it. But the frustration, the injustice... those feelings just took over. Why did her Dad hate her? She didn't care, she hated him too. Why did he only ever love Jackie? She, Nicola, wasn't wanted. She was sure of that. It was her fault that her mom had died. Those and other similar ideas passed vaguely through her mind.

*

"You coming, Nic?"

"Yeah, sure".

Everyone had Julie Wood marked out as trouble. The rumours flew around school that she had been pregnant at the age of 13.

She hadn't been pregnant at all. But Julie knew of the rumours and played up to them. She wore make-up to school, every day. And every day she was told to take it off. She wore jewellery, every day, and every day she was told to take that off too. And although the shops around the corner were out of bounds, she went to those every day too.

She also smoked. And she made it clear that she smoked. And that was where she was going now. To have a cigarette.

That involved a long walk across the flat grey concrete tennis courts. Then, at the last minute, rather than leave the school premises, ducking behind the bicycle sheds.

Nicola and Julie had been 'best friends' for a few years now.

But where Julie flirted and played with the boys, Nicola was dark and indifferent.

Julie wore her blouse partially unbuttoned. Nicola wore a black shirt. The school uniform was white blouses for girls. But Nicola, now a fifth year, didn't care for that. She wore black.

Julie wore whatever the latest fashion was, in terms of shoes. But Nicola wore boots. Black boots.

And although both girls were tall, Julie was naturally red-haired and proud of that, whereas Nicola, naturally almost black haired, went out of her way to darken her hair even more. Almost black wasn't enough. She wanted it to be jet black.

"Did you get it done?" asked Julie as the two girls crossed the playground.

"Yeah", said Nicola.

"How much was it?"

"Fifteen quid".

"Oh, that's not so bad", said Julie.

They turned left and went behind the bike sheds.

There were already two boys there. Both smoking. They glanced up at the 5th year girls but didn't say anything.

The school knew about the smoking. And, from time to time, a teacher did go to the bike sheds to tell a few kids off and maybe hand out a few detentions. But, in the main, it was easier to just let a few cigarettes go. Unofficially of course. This way, at least the smokers came back to class. If the school had pushed them, they would just have skipped school completely.

Julie took a packet of cigarettes out of her pocket. Nicola produced a lighter. One of those gaudy plastic ones. Each girl took a cigarette, lit it, and for a few drags, said nothing.

Finally Julie blew out a long thin trail of blue smoke. It circled wildly around for a moment in the light breeze and then, with a flick, shot away up and over the corrugated roof of the bike sheds.

"Let's have a look then", she said.

Nicola glanced at the two boys, then shrugged. She took off her black jumper, and pulled her black shirt off her pale shoulder to reveal a small tattoo of a snake, running partially under her bra strap.

"Oh", said Julie. "It's bigger than I thought it was going to be".

Nicola looked down at her own shoulder and nodded.

Then she pulled her shirt back up and covered the thing up.

"S'alright, though", she said.

And it was OK. It was quite a stylish tattoo, as those things go. And it suited Nicola. It matched very well with her often dark personality and her dark style.

"Are you going to get one done?" asked Nicola, lighting another cigarette.

Julie nodded. "Only little though", she said. "I want a rose. On my ankle".

"Oh, Jimmy will do that", said Nicola. "No bother. Probably only cost a fiver".

That evening, back at home, Nicola had a bath. Showers were more or less unheard of in those small red brick homes, and those which did exist were just cheap rubber things that attached to the bath taps but leaked furiously. And as Nicola sat in the bath, wanting a cigarette but not daring to light one up, she looked at herself, her shoulder and her tattoo in a mirror.

She smiled.

Nicola had grown into a stunning looking girl and she knew it. She had always been pretty, with those dark looks, but now she

was tall and well-proportioned and her face was good –
symmetrical, very attractive. Some boys told her that her eyes
were her best feature. Bright blue like a summer sky. Others
mentioned her legs. Others said that her breasts were her best
feature.

She laughed at that thought. Maybe she'd get a tattoo there next.

"Left or right?" she said to herself, weighing each as she did so.

Suddenly there was a knock at the bathroom door.

"What?" asked Nicola angrily. "What do you want? I'm in the
bath".

"You gonna be long?" It was Jackie.

Immediately Nicola changed her tone. "No, darling. I'll only be a
few minutes. Why? Do you need something?"

"No. It's alright", said Jackie. "I jus wanted to get a clean towel
out of the airing cupboard".

"Big or small?"

"Small".

Without hesitation, Nicola stood, got out of the bath, opened the
airing cupboard, dripping water and soap bubbles as she did so,
and reached in for a small towel. She unbolted the bathroom door

and, peering out to make sure that only Jackie was there, she passed her younger sister the towel.

"Oh", said Jackie, noticing the tattoo on Nicola's shoulder. "What's that? Can I see?"

Nicola lifted her shoulder and showed Jackie.

"A tattoo!" said Jackie. "When did you get that done?"

"At the weekend", Nicola replied.

"The weekend just gone?" asked Jackie.

Nicola nodded.

"Oh God", said Jackie, "Dad went crazy when you didn't come home".

"He shouldn't have had a go at me, then, should he? He's always going on at me".

"Is that when you got it done?" asked Jackie.

Nicola shrugged. And with a quick smile, she closed the bathroom door. Bolted it. Got back into the bath and ran some more hot water.

A week later, the first warmth of the year arrived. Those few days which, in March, can sometimes see the temperatures rise as high as 20°C. Nice enough to sit on the grass, in the sun. Warm enough to make summer feel near. But a false spring, really, as cold weather always returns before April.

It was on one of those days, doing the laundry for the three of them, and hanging the washing out, that Nicola stopped in the garden for the briefest of moments, wearing a white vest. White vest and black jeans.

She stood there and drew in a great breath of soft, fresh air.

She closed her eyes and remembered a spring day, like this, many years ago, when her mother had made a tent in the back garden from two old blankets and two kitchen chairs. Nicola and Jackie had sat in that tent, reading, talking and even having their tea out there, until the evening air turned cold.

"What's that on your arm?" interrupted the familiar voice from the open kitchen door.

The washing line was easily visible from that door. The back garden was very small.

"Shit", said Nicola to herself. She moved behind a sheet which billowed slightly in the barely moving breeze, quickly untying her black cardigan from around her waist, and putting it on.

"Nicola", said her father again. "Come here".

There was no back gate. No easy escape from that garden. Nicola had climbed across other gardens in the past, at night playing with friends. It was possible to escape. But, really, no. There was nothing for it. She would have to go back into the house. Through the kitchen and so past her father.

"That had better be a drawing, young lady", said her father as she entered the kitchen.

"It is", Nicola lied.

"You're not even sixteen".

Does that have anything to do with it? Nicola thought to herself. What does my age matter?

"Show me your arm", said her father.

Nicola sighed heavily. But slipped her shoulder out of her cardigan anyway.

"A bloody tattoo!"

Nicola shrugged. Pulled her cardigan back up and tried to go upstairs.

But her father wouldn't let it drop so easily.

And once again an argument quickly erupted.

"No daughter of mine is going to have a tattoo".

Then, "Who did it?"

Then, "You can get that taken off".

Then, "I'll go round there and see this bloody Jimmy".

And no matter what Nicola said, the thing just rolled on and on. And on.

Even when Nicola went upstairs, and started playing music as loudly as she could manage, the argument continued. There were more threats. There was some swearing. No violence, and somewhere deep inside, Nicola knew that her father probably didn't really mean any of it. Not most of it anyway.

But she could give as good as she got.

And when her father was still going on at her, almost an hour later, she finally told him to fuck off.

That was the point of no return.

Voices rose louder. Doors were slammed. Nicola was ordered to turn the music off. Nicola told him to fuck off again. And her father told her she had always been trouble and that he looked forward to the day she would leave home.

"Me too!" was Nicola's reply.

As they stood there in the hall, staring at each other with an unnecessary fury, the front door opened and Jackie came in. She had been out at her dance practice.

"What's going on?" she asked, visibly upset. "I can hear you two all the way up the street".

Nicola snorted. Then took one look at Jackie and calmed down immediately. "Nothing", she said. "It's nothing".

Jackie's arrival also helped soothe their father. Though, unlike Nicola, he took a little longer to calm down. And for quite a while longer, he went on to Jackie about how good she, Jackie, was and how much trouble Nicola was. And had always been.

But by now, Nicola had gone to bed.

*

"This is all there is", said Nicola. "There isn't anything else".

Nicola and Jackie were sitting in one of those 1950s estate pubs. The kind of place where people gathered after a funeral or, sometimes, where the function room would be hired for a wedding with a cold buffet of chicken drumsticks and sausage rolls.

Despite their functional design and often gaudy decor, on summer evenings, sitting in the car park, such pubs could be almost cheerful places. Families and friends, youngest to oldest, laughed and joked over poor quality – but cheap – beer. The sun setting low, cigarette ends rolling slowly across the grey tarmac and a growing aroma of fish and chips from the small group of shops nearby.

Big estates were not always dark, hostile and humourless.

By late autumn, however, things were often quite different. As the dark nights began to draw in, such pubs could become threatening and even dangerous. Not somewhere to visit unless you had grown up on that estate.

Nicola and Jackie had no such concerns. They were well known. Especially Nicola with her partially shaved head, tattoos and piercings. Everyone recognised her.

"If you're lucky", Nicola continued, lighting yet another cigarette, "you have a good childhood. Lots of love and toys and fun. You're good looking and you do well at school. Or you don't have those things. Either way, then you turn into a teenager, an adolescent".

She laughed and took a swig of her pint of lager.

"Look at me", she said, still laughing. "We all think we're the first person to do...whatever. We think no one else understands.

Has never felt the same. Generations come and go. And they all think that!"

"Alright girls", said a voice they didn't recognise. "Get you a drink?"

"No thanks", said Jackie.

Nicola just shook her head and carried on talking.

"That passes. Mostly. For most people. You date a bunch of different people and finally, without really knowing why, you settle down with one of them. Take each other for granted, usually, as the years go by. You have kids. Or not. It depends. If you have kids, you pass the whole rotten shit show onto them. And eventually you sit there in your armchair unable to walk properly any more, watching their lives. Trying to recreate your own existence through them and then through your grandchildren".

"And if you don't have kids?" asked Jackie.

Nicola shrugged.

"A career. You make ball bearings or vases or fucking something else we don't need. You fill our world with pointless stuff we don't really want and then one day you're fired. Or you're told you're too old and you're pensioned off. From then on you have holidays and rheumatism until you die. And it doesn't matter what you do, what you think or feel, it doesn't matter how you cut it up or what story you tell yourself. That's all there is."

Jackie laughed.

Every now and then Nicola would launch into a long, almost breathless rant against the world. The next day, in all likelihood, she would be going to a party somewhere and singing as she got ready to go out.

"Will you get married?" Nicola asked, suddenly.

Jackie thought about it for a while and then nodded. "Yes. I think so. I hope so. I'd be quite happy to have kids and then grandchildren."

Nicola took another cigarette out of the packet. Hesitated, then put it back in the packet again. "Good", she said. "I'd like to be an aunt".

For the next half an hour, two lads off the estate sat with the two girls, trying, in the main, to chat up Nicola.

Finally, the boys gave up and left.

"Sex", said Nicola. "Even that's a fucking joke. Sex. A big so fucking what. You have shit sex or you have great sex and feel that the world has connected two of you together. But it hasn't. Not really. Sooner or later the magic will fade."

"Or the retirement and rheumatism will get you?"

"Both! A world without magic is one with rheumatism!"

An hour or so later, having put the world to rights on several scores, the two girls left the pub.

"Shall we go to the chippy?" asked Nicola.

"Go on then", said Jackie. "But only if I can have a small packet of chips. I don't want a whole one."

It didn't take long to get served, as it was a quiet Tuesday night.

"I'll walk up with you", said Nicola, opening her chips and starting to eat them.

"No, I'm fine", said Jackie. "There's no need". Jackie didn't open her chips. She was saving them so she could put them on a plate to eat them.

"No", said Nicola. "Don't worry, I'm not coming in. Not if he's there. But I'll walk you back."

So that was what she did.

They walked up the hill together, until just a few metres short of the gate, where Jackie stopped.

Nicola had left home ages ago. But Jackie still lived there.

"Nic..." she said, hesitantly. "Can I ask you something?"

With a mouthful of chips, Nicola nodded.

"About our dad."

"Yeah?"

"It's a funny thing to ask", said Jackie, a little awkwardly.

Nicola shrugged.

"Do you think you'll ever make it up with him?"

Nicola shook her head. "No. I don't think so. We've tried. But he always winds me up the wrong way, and I suppose I must do the same to him".

Jackie nodded.

"Nothing ever happened, did it? I mean, when we were little".

Nicola's big blue eyes widened. "God, no. No. Nothing. No. It was nothing like that. Not at all."

Jackie nodded again. And then smiled. "I'd better go in. These chips will be cold."

"OK."

Jackie fumbled for her key and finally found it. She half turned to her sister and said, "And take care walking home".

But Nicola had already gone.

*

Guildford wasn't the sort of place that sprung to mind when thinking about rebellion. A bright but, in many respects, dreary suburban town in Surrey, it was somewhere that stockbrokers lived. A place with golf clubs and lads who drank too much lager on the weekend.

Middle England is full of these places. Too big to be rural, too impersonal to care. Too small to be thrusting, too small to be tough.

Young people leave places like Guildford – they don't move there.

But, then, Nicola hadn't exactly moved there.

Wrought iron gates and a wooden fence at the end of a cul-de-sac, *that* was moving there. Walking the dog, buying a huge flat screen TV, washing the car, *that* was moving there. Nicola wasn't doing any of those things. She was living in a multi-storey car-park in the town centre.

It wasn't her first choice of residence. But, then again, neither was it as bad as the squat she had just left.

That squat, situated between Clapham and Brixton in south London had nothing at all to recommend it. Nicola had met a boy, two years younger than her, who lived there, and so she had moved in. Having nowhere else to go right then, the decision had made some sense.

But the place was bedlam. Not just noise, which both Nicola and Jock – the boy – could have handled. But bedlam in terms of the people and the things they did.

A good squat had a more or less settled population. An owner who left the people alone. Neighbours who did the same. It could be a bolt hole, away from the pain and madness of homelessness, which would serve for maybe as much as 18 months.

But a bad squat was like an open sore. The owner – or his relatives – would cause trouble. Threats or actual violence. Crash into the place at any hour. Neighbours could do the same. One night, a berserk man with an axe smashed up the entire downstairs of the squat. The police didn't give a damn. The man paid his rates and taxes. The squatters did not.

More than that, the population of this particular squat wasn't steady, not settled. Instead it was a rapidly alternating tangle of people who crashed there to use drugs before disappearing forever, or who hid there, as a group of eight or more did, for ten days while the police looked elsewhere for them.

"Let's get out of here", said Jock one day, having come 'home' to the squat to find his few meagre possessions gone. "There's got to be better places than this".

The two of them, Nicola and Jock, then spent a few nights sleeping under a railway arch. Pestered by punters at night – because of Nicola's looks mainly, but some of them would have happily used Jock too – and pestered during the day by the council who were adamant that this, this particular railway arch, was not a "suitable" place to live. As if Nicola and Jock had ever believed that it was.

On top of that, they had already been around the south London squat circuit for the last year or so and it felt flat. Very flat. Not just in terms of music or youth culture, but this was also a time where a caring government made an issue out of people sleeping rough. Should they be fined? one newspaper asked. Should they be moved out of London to another town? asked another.

"Let's do that", said Nicola, reading that same newspaper at 3 am because that night someone was sobbing only a few cardboard box beds away.

"What?" asked Jock. He would be 20 soon.

"Let's go and do this, sleep rough, but in a little rural town somewhere instead".

Jock lit a cigarette, smoked it for a while, then passed it to Nicola. She took a few drags, then passed it back to Jock.

"Be homeless in a county town?" laughed Jock.

"Why not?" asked Nicola.

Of course such small towns already had their own homeless. The UK was like that. But they were – surely? – safer and somewhat easier than London. At least, that was how Nicola and Jock saw things that cold, wet, tear-filled night.

So the next day, having cadged a few pounds to travel a stop or two on a train, that was what they did.

They caught a train. Stayed on longer than their tickets allowed. And were finally thrown off at Guildford.

Neither Nicola nor Jock knew the town at all. And they didn't know anyone who lived there.

But, hanging around on the streets, with Jock's brightly coloured mohican and with Nicola's piercings, tattoos and now partially shaven head... it didn't take them long to attract attention and become quite well known.

Guildford wasn't London, Birmingham or Manchester. But it still had students, and it still had a few rebels. And in no time at all, Jock and Nicola were sleeping on the floor of a man's house. He, Adam, was a decent man. He worked for the BBC, in the sound department, where he particularly enjoyed mixing strange special effects. But at the weekend, or when not working, he also helped to put events on in the little town. Gigs, mainly. But there was also the odd larger event. Guildford even had its own small festival.

If Nicola had wanted to stay there, on that floor, indefinitely, Adam would almost certainly have let her. That wasn't because he had a thing about her – Adam was gay – but it was because she could be quiet. Quiet in the sense that she knew when to shut up and go to bed. Jock, by contrast, would often keep Adam up until the silly hours, talking incessantly while taking speed and weed.

More than that, Nicola, for all that she was homeless, still retained all her manners and habits of cleanliness and so forth, which made her a pleasure to have around. Now and then, for who knew what reason, she might be darkly moody. But there was nothing depressing or down in those moods. She could just be... dark. There was no other word for it.

Jock, by contrast, had to reminded from time to time to wash his clothes or even himself. And slowly, but surely, over a six month stay, those small habits of Jock's became an annoyance to Adam.

And not only to Adam. To Nicola too. Nicola, who liked Jock, who slept with him – though less often than Jock wanted – who saw in him the good man he really was, was also becoming annoyed with his more or less anti-social ways. And moving out from Adam's seemed the best way to change the mechanics of the situation.

It was early summer. Both Nicola and Jock were reasonably content in Guildford. They were familiar faces. By now, they even had a few friends. Why not spend the summer sleeping rough?

Wasn't that what they had left London to try out?

"Be homeless in a county town".

"Where will you go?" asked Adam. "You're not leaving town?"

Nicola shook her head.

"The multi storey", said Jock. "We've already crashed there a few times. I like it there. I've always had a thing about multi-storey car parks".

Adam glanced at Nicola, who was wearing a very loose white vest. Somewhere along the way, she had finally gotten one of her breasts tattooed. That had been done following another argument with her father. (Though never, not once, not even to herself, did she admit to any connection between getting a tattoo and having such an argument).

"You can always come back here, to wash and so on", said Adam, kindly.

Sure enough, for the next couple of weeks, Nicola and Jock lived in the multi-storey car park in Guildford.

Nicola washed – and even shaved her legs – in a tiny metal sink in the public toilet in the car park.

One day, whilst she was doing that, wearing only her underwear, a man came into the ladies' by mistake. Nicola looked at him, shrugged and went back to shaving her legs. The man, an elderly chap in his 70s, wearing a blazer, was aghast. But he said nothing. Simply turned and left.

Quite what he made of a young, almost naked, tattooed and pierced woman, in her underwear, shaving her legs in a tiny metal sink in the multi-story car park... that was hard to tell.

But a few days later the public toilets were locked.

And that made life in the car park that little bit harder.

The good thing about the car park – the best thing – was that on warm summer nights, Jock and Nicola could sleep on the top, with only the stars and each other for company. The security guards knew they were there, but to their credit left the pair of them to it.

It was on one of those nights, smoking a joint donated by a friend of Adam's, and having just made love under the moonlit sky, that Nicola told Jock she wanted to move on.

"Leave Guildford?" he said.

Nicola nodded.

"I don't want to leave", said Jock.

Nicola closed her eyes and counted out loud to seven.

"Shooting star", she said, opening her eyes again. "They're supposed to be lucky".

"I don't want to leave here", said Jock again. "I like it here. We're doing OK".

Nicola took the joint from Jock's fingers, smoked it quietly for a while, then shook her head. Took another draw, then stubbed out the last of it.

"Just me", she said. "I want to move on. From here, but from you too."

It wasn't an easy conversation to have. Goodbye conversations are never easy, even where circumstances are much more 'normal'. And for a while Jock protested, naturally enough.

But Nicola was adamant. "It's not you, it's not even Guildford. It's just me. Or life or something. I need to move on. Go somewhere else".

If Jock had been both more observant and much more honest with himself, the news that Nicola wanted away, out, anywhere, wouldn't have been a surprise. Time with her was borrowed time. There was something inside Nicola that wasn't going to settle. If ever, then not for many more years to come.

But, despite his multi-coloured mohican, Jock wasn't that restless. Wasn't in that place. Not the same place as Nicola. And he probably never would be.

"Where?" he finally managed to ask.

Nicola shrugged. "Brighton. At least to begin with."

Jock felt the anger rise. "That's where Andy comes from. You're just fucking going back to him".

After leaving school at the age of 16, having obtained a few certificates far below the levels her intellect deserved, Nicola had met a dazzling man named Andy, who had then been in his early 30s. It was her first summer of freedom, and Andy was in the process of moving to France. He had bought an old barn and wanted to move there and renovate it.

Nicola had gone with him. Without a word to anyone, except for Jackie. And, for a while, it had been romantic. Fun, sunshine, no cares. But the whole experience had turned out badly. Andy spent most of his money on drugs – not building materials. And before 12 months were out, Nicola was back in the UK. She had told Jock some of this when they first met. She had also told him that she still had a huge crush on Andy.

Jock had not felt troubled by that news. After all, Andy was 'lost in France', somewhere or other.

But the news had filtered down the grapevine, six months earlier, that Andy was once more in the UK. And living again in his home town of Brighton.

Was that why Nicola was heading there?

She said not.

Akeem's story

"Security forces would often crack down on demonstrations. So we always stayed indoors. It wasn't that we didn't want things to change, it was just that we were too frightened to get involved.

"For us, I mean, my wife, my children, me, things were actually very good anyway. I had qualified many years before as a civil engineer, worked in Saudi and even Germany for over ten years, before returning home to start a family. I was doing really well in Syria. My family were doing really well. But very many people were not, and we saw that. Most people, in fact. We knew lots of people who worked but couldn't afford a home, couldn't afford to get married until they were almost 40, couldn't even afford to eat properly or pay their bills.

"The regime itself was very good to some but it was also hard on others. It was rare – but not unheard of – for someone to be arrested and kept for a long time. In our own neighbourhood, that did not happen, but in others, certainly it did.

"So when change appeared to be coming, across all of the Arab world, we welcomed it in Syria too. It isn't right and it isn't sustainable for a few to do well at the expense of friends and neighbours.

"For most, at least at first, it wasn't about regime change or revolution or anything like that. Not at all. I'm sure there were some who wanted that, yes, but for most it was just about equality. It was all about making some changes, some reforms. Just some. People wanted the regime to modernise, you know. To become fairer. Kinder. That really was how it began for most people. The talk, before any street protests took place, was about reforms, not anything more.

"But even during the first demonstrations, the government took a tough stance. The crowds were mostly peaceful; certainly they were unarmed. Everyone hoped the regime would offer those reforms. But the government used teargas and water cannons against people. There were many arrests too.

"I really believe that if, from early on, the regime had given some ground and shown some kindness, things could have been halted early on. Instead the heavy-handedness just caused more unrest – and more demonstrations. People who only wanted improvement became 'activists' instead.

"More protests happened, and eventually the government started to use live ammunition. At first they fired over the crowds, but then they fired into the crowds. That was shocking. Horrible. And from that point on things quickly escalated and soon regime change seemed to be the only way.

"One night, security forces took the people from a house just across the street from our own. There was screaming and crying. I knew them. We all knew them. We had no idea why the police took them away. By the time they came back, two weeks later, they looked 50 years older.

"On another occasion, after a good deal of wild banging and shouting, we opened our back door to let two young girls into our home. They were only about 12 years old. And they were terrified. They had run along the alleyway, at the back of our house, crying, hammering on different doors, looking for somewhere to hide. We opened our door and they came in. The security forces were looking for them, too.

"Why?" my wife asked. "What have you done?"

"They have killed our father", one girl replied. "So we threw stones at them".

"We did not want to get involved. But what could we do? We let them in, closed the door and told them to remain quiet. My wife gave them something to drink but they were too scared to take anything. They were only young girls.

"The security forces started to hunt. Door to door. They did not find those girls, because they left by our front door, as security troops came in the back. But then the government forces turned our house upside down.

"Then the house next door... an elderly man, who had been a teacher all his life, and who had recently lost his wife, the security services entered his property and began smashing his home to pieces. We could hear them shouting and things being broken.

"At first we wanted to just stay indoors. Hide. But my wife told me I have to go and help. To stop the 'Shabiha', the militia, from destroying our neighbour's home. Others, too, faces from along the street, ordinary men and women, we all tried to stop the violence on that night. But we could not. And some of us were punched and beaten.

"Here, you have to remember that this was our own country. Where we had grown up, gone to school. We had lived and worked there all our lives and now, suddenly, our own army and police were attacking us. They were supposed to protect us, but now they were smashing up our homes.

"It was like a nightmare. In no time at all, we had gone from living a normal life, work, school, a car, plans for holidays... all the things you probably take for granted, and we had turned into a country being torn apart by a kind of war.

"For a while longer, things continued to be more or less normal. We tried to go to work and, often, we did so. But sometimes a car bomb would explode or a fight would break out. And going to work became impossible.

"The same for school, of course. We wanted our children to continue their schooling but the country was becoming a war zone. Schools closed. We tried to teach them at home, but it was not easy. Not at all.

"Soon it became impossible to know who to trust or when to trust them. One day, a government force would be generous. They would escort us through the streets. Show us a great deal of kindness. Then things would change. And there would be violence. Sometimes by government forces, sometimes by those who opposed the regime. A house that flew a Syrian flag would be attacked and ransacked by those was wanted change. A house that flew a 'rebel' flag would be attacked and ransacked by the government side. If you flew neither flag – if you tried to just stay out of things – that did not work either.

"Some of the rebel leaders began to line their own pockets. Some of the government forces did the same. All the time, ordinary people were on the receiving end.

"One day I was prevented from going to work by a rebel force. They told me they would kidnap me and demand a ransom unless I stayed at home. Another day, I saw two men – who were nothing to do with the rebels – dragged from their home and beaten to death in the street by the security forces. There was always gunfire.

"That was when the international community got involved. I don't mean in the sense that they stopped the fighting, but that they made it worse. Down on the ground, we didn't even know who was up there or why, but the bombs began falling. One day on forces belonging to the regime. The next day on forces fighting for change. It was complete madness.

"Still, all of us, we tried to live what you might call normal lives. But when houses in the street were hit by bombs and turned into rubble, when food and drink began to run out, what could we do? We fled the city. We had to leave behind our TVs, our beds, our clothes and all of that. Everything.

"Perhaps, in a way, we were luckier than some. Because my wife's family was quite wealthy, and they had a nice home, with spare rooms, out in the countryside in a little village called B_____. And so we went there. My wife, myself and our two children.

"In the countryside, at first, things were better. We had food again. And no bombs fell. There were no riots. But it was horrible to know that, back there, in the city, our home and our friends and neighbours were still exposed to all that pain.

"Slowly, though, even in the countryside, things began to become harder too. For a few days, the shops ran out of food. There were security checkpoints. We had no petrol. Then even our car was taken away. Some rebels escaped a fight and dug into the land just outside our village. They dug tunnels in the fields, and made trenches. I had read about the First World War in Europe, and it seemed to me that what had happened there was now happening in Syria.

"For ten days, all of us in the village had to remain indoors. What food we had, we made it last. Bullets were flying all over the place. But, fortunately, neither side bombed or shelled the village itself. By the time the security services and militia banged on our doors to tell us we could come out, countless men and women were dead in our fields and gardens.

"And then, in the escalating chaos, ISIS arrived."

*

"No one knew who or what ISIS were.

"Were they fighting for the government? Were they a new militia? Were they on the side of the rebels and fighting for regime change? We did not know.

"Wearing all black, they came into our village and, at first, they gave us food. They told us that from here on, we would be safe.

"There were not very many of them. They drove out of the village again, leaving a small pile of food and some Western food in tins.

They told us that they would maintain peace in the area where we were now living.

"It felt like a huge relief.

"And for a few days, things were almost back to normal. But, of course, we could not return home to the city. We were now living off the land as our grandfathers had done.

"ISIS came back to our village a few times during the next month or so. I talked to a few of the young men. They were all Syrians, who seemed so committed to their cause. I asked them who they were fighting for and they said they wanted to create a new country, in the Middle East, one that would be run as a proper Islamic state.

"To us, to my family, that sounded a very disturbing idea. We were Muslims, but we were not practicing Muslims. Life in Syria had taken us far away from religion. I told the ISIS soldiers this and they assured me everything would be fine. I think they really did believe that. But then, quite quickly, other ISIS fighters appeared. Very many more. And they had much more radical ideas.

"Again I spoke to one of them. He told me that the protests against the regime were being manipulated by America and that the regime itself was being propped up by Russia. And that neither side would back down until Syria – and Iraq and other countries too – were almost wiped out. They, the Russians and Americans, wanted to crush us.

"He said these words with a passion. He really believed what he was saying. And, perhaps, he was right. It was certainly true that Syria was now being torn in two. That what had begun as an internal struggle had now become an international conflict.

"But it was not that which worried me. I felt sure, as most of us did, that things would calm down sooner or later – with or without Russian and American intervention. What worried me now was this drive to create a single Islamic country. There had not been such a thing for hundreds of years. We all lived together in peace. Some people were passionate Muslims, some were Christian and so forth. And many of us were not like that. We lived a more or less Western lifestyle. Live and let live. That was all we wanted. But ISIS did not want that. And it soon became apparent that they were worse – much worse – than anything we had known beforehand.

"The first bad thing ISIS did was divide the villagers up. Those who they considered to be religious, or true believers, and those who they considered not to be religious. We, my family, were in the latter group.

"The 'true believers' were given money, food, and told to make sure that the rest of us began living according to strict Sharia law. Some of them did not want to do this, but some of them did. People, even families, began turning against each other. I had read all about the Holocaust, and I could see, straight away, that the same thing was going to happen here. When you begin to turn friends and neighbours against each other, that is what happens.

"My uncle was arrested – on the word of one of the 'true believers' – and taken away by ISIS soldiers. He was beaten, electrocuted, tortured. He finally came back to us, very frail. He died within a matter of days.

"Then ISIS began taking women away. There were some women in the village who were not Muslim. They were taken away. Any resistance was met with violence and even, in one case, a man was shot and killed in the main street of the village. His body was left lying there and ISIS took his wife away. They told the rest of us that unless we did what they said, unless we obeyed all their rules, to the letter, they would come back for more.

"It was like living in mediaeval times.

"Only six months before, we had been playing video games on our TV and talking about our holiday plans.

"That is how war changes things.

"One day, we received a letter from my wife's mother. Normally letters and any other form of communication were blocked, one way or another. We lived cut off from everything. And we knew that others, other villages and towns, must have been experiencing the same thing.

"But this one letter, smuggled in by a friend, did reach us.

"It confirmed that ISIS were now ruling over great swathes of Syria and neighbouring countries. And that they were torturing and murdering many people in order to create their new religious state.

"That was when I decided to get my wife and children away. Out of there and to safety. I had spoken to them before, about going, but they had not wanted to leave me, leave their family and friends. But now it was clear – they had to go.

"Smuggling your children out of their own home is not an easy thing to do.

"But we had some money and one of the most important villagers, who ISIS respected, was a very close friend of the family.

"It took a lot of planning, and it was a horrible thing to do, but in the end we managed it. My wife, my two children, and another family, were all taken away by Land Rover, at the dead of night, to a safe place.

"Those next few days, waiting to hear, were the worst days of my life.

"But finally we heard from them. All of them had safely crossed the border into Turkey – aided by Kurds.

"At that time, I think there was no one we could trust in our country any more. Only the Kurds seemed to be trustworthy. Only they seemed to be fighting for what was right. Everyone else – government supporters, rebels, ISIS, American, Russians, Turks... all seemed to be fighting for themselves now. But that was not so of the Kurds. We heard only good of them.

"Within a few weeks, I heard again from my wife and children. They had made it to Britain. We had some, few, family members there and they had pressed the British government to help us. At first the British had not wanted to, but an uncle had some influential friends who donated money to the ruling Conservative party – and one thing followed another.

"With my family out of the village and safe in England, I felt a little better. A little less scared. And so I, too, began to look for ways that I could help others. It felt like the only thing to do. The right thing to do. To try to save my country from this chaos."

*

"Every now and then, ISIS would visit the village and arrest or detain some people. Always, at first, people who were not Muslim or who, like me, were not considered to be religious. I don't know why they left me alone, but they did. Perhaps that was because of that same friend of the family.

"Some people disappeared, never to be seen again. Others came back with a mutilated hand, or perhaps a leg missing. Anything and everything.

"It was obvious, to me anyway, that it was only a question of time before they did the same to me. So I left the village. I ran. And I joined up with a group of Kurds who were fighting against ISIS – and others. I had been a civil engineer, now I was a guerrilla soldier. I just wanted my old life back, but what could I do?

"Through the Kurdish group, we rescued many men, women and children who would otherwise have been captured by ISIS and tortured and killed.

"Sometimes, of course, some of our own people were killed. But we all felt it was a price worth paying.

"The bravest Kurds were often women. I had barely met a Kurd before all the troubles began, but now I felt proud of them. We fought for others and we hoped that, once the war was done, the international community would help all of us too. Give the Kurds their own homeland.

"On one mission, my seventh, a small group of us were to ambush ISIS at a bridge. It was a place they always used. They always took prisoners via this same route to their prisons. We had rescued some American journalists at this very spot only a month beforehand.

"But this time, someone, somewhere, betrayed us.

"There was a short fire fight. We lost. I wanted to die there and then rather than be captured by ISIS, but that did not happen. And I was captured by them.

"I was thrown into one of their vehicles, blindfolded and handcuffed, and then taken to one of their bases where I was beaten and interrogated from dawn until after darkness fell.

"This continued for a number of days. I told them nothing, not because I was a brave man, but because there was nothing I could tell them.

"I was jailed with dozens of other men in a large bare concrete room. We slept on the bare floor and were watched by cameras. Our food, such as it was, consisted of a few slices of stale bread, a rotten potato or two and an egg. There was one tap with which we had to wash and from which we drank.

"None of my Kurdish friends were there.

"Everyone in the room was Muslim. I was sure – we were all sure – that anyone else, everyone who was not Muslim, had been taken away and killed.

"ISIS only spared Muslims. And, even then, not all Muslims. I saw some detainees taken, tortured with electric shocks and then brought back. Others never returned.

"This went on for a few months, I became thin, tired, unable to sleep, and then, suddenly, one day, the day after I had received a long and vicious beating, I was released. Just like that.

"I was made to sign a few documents – to confess my guilt – which I was barely able to sign because I was so weak, and then I was released.

"Apparently our old family friend, from the village, had paid over a large sum of money for my release.

"I was lucky. Very lucky. Without his help, I am sure I would have been beaten to death or I would have died of hunger or disease in that awful place.

"That was when, I suppose, the strangest of things happened.

"ISIS released me, dozens of miles from anywhere I could call home, and they told me to go back to the village.

"But they made no attempt to force me to do so.

"There was no transport. I had no money. Nothing.

"At first I began walking, more or less in the direction of my village. But then I thought 'No, Why should I do what they tell me? No. I will not go back to my village. I will go to England. I will escape this madness and go to England and my family'.

"Much of Syria is empty space. As soon as I walked away from the road, there was nothing. No one.

"And so, as darkness arrived, I just lay down and slept where I was. I could hear ISIS vehicles, shouting and gunfire from where I lay. But they were not looking for me. They had already forgotten about me.

"I woke very early the next day. Absolutely starving. I did not think I would be able to survive another day without rest and food. But I did survive.

"I walked. I ate a few green leaves. I drank some bitter water. I found a fruit tree and ate all I could. And, somehow, I kept going.

I walked in the direction of the Kurds. Always expecting to hear the crack of a rifle and then to fall down dead. But nothing happened.

"Maybe, if people saw me, they just took pity. I don't know. I must have looked like a scarecrow. I was ragged and thin. Dirty. I had no idea what day it was, nor the date. Nothing.

"All around me, I knew, were ISIS and Kurdish fighter groups. Surely, I thought, someone soon will stop me. But no. And then I realised that there was a big battle being fought, some miles to the east, and so perhaps they were all too occupied with that.

"I kept walking. I had reached the state of mind where I almost did not care what happened. If someone had shot me, I would not have cared – except I wanted to see my wife and children again. That was the only thing that kept me going.

"Finally, what must only have been a dozen or so miles from safety in the Kurdish sector, I heard a gunshot and some voices. People shouting at me. They fired over my head. I stopped. I hoped, expected even, that they would be Kurds. But they were not. It was an ISIS jeep. I had been caught by them again.

"This ISIS group took me to their camp. It was back in the same direction I had just walked with so much pain and difficulty. That was the moment I thought I would certainly die. There was no escape, I told myself.

"At the camp, I was pushed around, hit a few times, interrogated. They asked me who I was, and what I was doing so close to the Kurdish front lines. I hardly had any words to answer them, so I just showed them my release document and told them I was lost. I said 'I think I have gone the wrong way'.

"I thought they would kill me but instead they just laughed. They said I was an idiot. And then, to my surprise, they gave me food and drink.

"I was in that camp for a week or so before more fighting broke out. ISIS would not let me go, but nor did they torture me. I think they were too pre-occupied with the Kurds and the fighting.

"Then there was a battle. Bullets hit a big metal container, to which I had been very loosely bound. There were holes all around my head but I was not hit. It occurred me that one of the very worst things about war, about this whole madness, was that you could feel one day that you were fated to survive, that nothing was going to touch you, and the next day you would feel the very opposite. You would whimper and cry like a dog. Certain that you were doomed. War does that. It is chaos. Pure and simple. You do not know what will happen next.

"The fighting raged for a few days and then the camp emptied. Suddenly and dramatically. ISIS left and the Kurds arrived. I knew none of them, but they released me anyway. If I was a prisoner of ISIS, then in their eyes, whoever I was, that made me worthy of release.

"Once again I walked towards the Turkish border. But this time, with some food and drink inside me, I made it. I walked up a mountain, down the other side, and I asked a man with a donkey where I was. And he told me I was in Turkey."

*

"All I wanted to do was find my wife and children. Everything else had been lost. All sense had gone from the world.

"But, strangely, the first thing I had to do was leave Turkey. I had to leave, and go back into Syria. There I could buy a fake ID which would allow me to come back into Turkey legally. More or less legally.

"To get the money, I had to ask some Kurds. I talked to them about who I was, how I had fought with them, and they were very helpful. The fake ID was not expensive by Western standards, only about 30 American dollars. But it took a few days for them to get me that money and the card.

"So it was that I entered Turkey for a second time. I knew no one in that country. Not really. But the situation on the border was quite fluid and so, with a little patience, it was possible to get away and into the country proper. To find a small farm and eat. To work for a few days and eat. To travel a little and slowly.

"Like very many others, tens of thousands of us, I had become a wandering labourer. Lost in a foreign country. And all because of a war that no one really understood.

"But from my time in Syria, in the city, in the village, as a fighter and as a prisoner, I had become tougher. Where before I would have felt afraid, I had now lost my sense of fear. It came at times, for the strangest of reasons, but mostly it was gone. I was immune to it. I had one goal and nothing else mattered. Even if it took years, I would cross from Turkey into Europe, and cross from Europe to England.

"I had some friends who had settled in Bulgaria and, through a Turkish engineering school – where I had once presented a paper

– I was able to make contact with them. They invited me to join them. I only possessed fake documents. I was not sure if I could get there. But, in fact, it turned out that I could. Once again it was just a question of buying a fake document. And so that was what I did.

"Using that document, and paying more money at different places, I left Turkey for Bulgaria. I had to promise I was only visiting as a tourist and that I would leave in two weeks. Of course that was a lie. I had already been in Turkey for four months, at this point, and I had received no contact from my family. I no longer knew where they were. And I had no way of finding them short of travelling to England.

"With the help of my friends, I crossed from Bulgaria to Romania as easily as a man walks through an open door. And in Romania, once again, I worked at one labouring job after another.

"On the farms we were woken before the sun had risen. We worked in fields until our backs were rigid and our fingers bled with the cold. It was not war, and I was glad of that, but it was the hardest job I had ever known or seen. It was horrible.

"When one short term job finished, we were moved to another. And so it went on. I tried to leave the group I was working with, but I was told in no uncertain terms that if I left, I would probably be caught and shot. It was then I realised that I had fallen into some sort of forced labour group, organised by criminal gangs.

"I began to wonder if the whole world had gone mad. Was there nowhere left that people still treated each other with respect and dignity?

"Of course I tried to escape – and I was caught. But they did not shoot me. That was just a threat. And so I escaped again.

"In a small Romanian town, I found some other people from Syria. They organised demonstrations in Romania, Austria and Germany to keep things in the public eye. They spoke to the media about the goals of those who wanted to change the regime and about the regime's criminal practices against the Syrian people.

"I was shocked to hear some of their stories about things the regime had done. It was hard to listen to how badly others had been treated while some of us had been doing so well.

"They spoke about ISIS too. About the atrocities being committed by ISIS in the name of Islam. But they were confident that ISIS would soon be gone. For them, that would bring the whole war full circle, back to the Syrian regime.

"The aim would be once again to push for a peaceful revolution, to reveal the truth of what was happening inside Syria and how the regime was oppressing and torturing protesters in detention centres.

"I worked with these people for a while, and also saved some money for myself. It was amazing the things they did. They bought old ambulances from Germany and equipped them with stretchers and wheelchairs and then drove them to Syria.

"In total, over a period of a few years, they sent more than 50 second-hand ambulances to Syria, buying them from across Europe with money earned or donated by Syrians in exile. It was a wonderful effort to help our own people.

"On one occasion, in the middle of winter, two ambulances were brought over the mountains from Austria. Conditions were particularly hard and there was an accident during a heavy snowstorm at the most dangerous part of the journey. Help was needed and I was on hand. We received a phone call and drove out to the mountains. The ambulances were on a back road, of course, and stuck in deep snow with more falling all the time. For over 12 hours we struggled to free them. One of them had slid off the road. But finally we did manage to free them, and once in Bucharest, the Romanian capital, they were loaded with medical supplies to be driven to Syria to aid the men and women who were fighting there against the regime and against ISIS.

"We had no international aid money to help us. This work was all done voluntarily and when I later discovered just how much money was being poured into my country, from opposing global forces, I was horrified. Here we were struggling to provide basic supplies, struggling sometimes to find a few dollars and yet millions of dollars' worth of weapons were being used on my country as if money was unimportant.

"I think it was then that I realised however much good we were doing, our home had become some sort of pawn, a small piece in a crazy chess game. And I saw that I just wanted out. I wanted my life back again. I wanted to see my wife and children again. It had now been two years since I had seen them.

"But then I fell ill. Since rescuing those ambulances from the snow, I had had a bad chest infection, one that I could not shake off. For some months I kept working, trying to be of some use, but also trying to save some money so that I could continue my journey to England. But I was exhausted and I fell seriously ill.

"I don't really remember what happened, exactly. One day I was working, the next I was in a makeshift hospital. I could not be treated properly by the Romanian system because I was there illegally.

"I spent some months in that place, going in and out of consciousness at first for a long time. My friends were very worried about me, and one doctor said that I might not recover. But the mind is stronger than the body and I wanted to see my family. I felt guilty about being in Romania while my children were so far away. And suddenly nothing else mattered.

"With that single thought in my mind, I did get well. I spent a few more weeks recovering and then decided it was time to start moving again.

"Some Syrian friends of mine, in Romania, received a phone call telling them that they had been accepted by the Netherlands. That they could move there, legally. I had not been accepted. I had no connection with the Netherlands. But they were adamant they would take me on their journey. And that was what they did.

"Once more, as had been the case for so long now that I could hardly remember doing otherwise, I bought fake documents and travelled on those. Because we were already inside Europe, border checks were not so tough. And after a fairly long and tiring few days' drive, we all arrived in the Dutch capital of Amsterdam."

*

"I spent about six months in and around Amsterdam, working when I could. But it was not easy to find work there without the right papers. Eventually I fell in with some men who worked at the docks of Rotterdam. Almost all work there was very carefully checked, but there was some work, on the periphery, where illegal immigrants were needed. And so I became friends with men who knew all about the ships that crossed the sea every day to England.

"Back in Amsterdam, I asked Syrian aid groups and others to help find news of my family. The last time I had heard from them, they were in Nottingham but moving. Where to? My family had not been sure. They were going to let me know as soon as they had news. But, of course, that news never arrived.

"The months passed and, try as they might, the aid groups had no news about my family. I was already exhausted and anxious, worried. But now I felt desperate too. What could I do? How had things come to this?

"One day, talking to my friends in the port, one of them told me that the only thing for me was to cross, as soon as possible, to England. They could see that I was, slowly but surely, beginning to go crazy with the worry and fear. They told me I had to go. And they were right.

"One ship was leaving for a French port the next day, and, they told me, I would be able to board it quite easily. Even without any papers. I asked them what good it would do me to enter a French port. And they assured me that, because I had arrived in the port on a boat from Holland, it would be possible to transfer onto another ship, one bound for England, without going through any sort of customs or other checks.

"'Will you do it?' they asked me. Well. It was sudden. But I did not care. I wanted to go. So I said, 'Yes'. And arrangements were made that night.

"The next day I caught that boat. No paperwork. Nothing. It took me to the little French port of Dieppe. Security at the port was very slight. Once there, one of the crew, a Syrian who now lived legally in the Netherlands, transferred me onto a small and rusty ship carrying fishing equipment to the south coast of England.

"It smelt terrible. And the sea was very rough. But I did not care. Not at all. Because in a matter of hours I knew that, at last, I would be in the same country as my wife and children. It felt as if the nightmare was finally going to end.

"We arrived at Newhaven very early in the morning. To make sure they did not get into trouble, the crew of the boat informed police officers and customs officials of my presence. They said I had smuggled myself on board. I was happy for them to do this because I knew it was for the best and I did not want them to get into any trouble.

"I had to tell my story many times to the British authorities. Very many times. And when they asked about my family I had to tell the truth; I did not know where they were. It was hard to tell other men this. It felt wrong. I felt like I had failed. I was ashamed of myself. I did not know where my own children were.

"Very soon afterwards I was moved into temporary accommodation on the outskirts of Brighton."

Lori's story

Robert played Wagner's Tannhauser Overture so often and so loudly.

Lori had often seen tears in Robert's eyes as he listened to it.

This was the man she had waited her entire life for. He was passionate. Creative, yet practical too. He had enough money to be comfortable. And more than anything else, he was kind.

Sure, he was 50 now, ageing, but he had kept slim and fit. And with a shaved head and greying whiskers, when he wore his Yves St Laurent suit, Robert looked every inch a film director. Heads turned in the street. At both of them. And for all the right reasons.

Lori watched Robert as he listened to the overture again.

All her life. For this man. This one man. How was she so sure this was him? Because Lori was transgender and Robert was the first man, ever, in all of her 45 years, who had totally accepted her for who she was. No questions. No problems. No issues. For the first time in her life, Lori had met a man who didn't see her as a fantasy – a man who was proud to date her, to hold her hand in public. All of it. Any of it.

She looked at Robert again. The music reached a crescendo and she laughed. She laughed and lay back on the mattress and lit a joint.

She had given up believing in God, in good luck, in fortune, she had given up believing in everything and then, almost by accident, Robert had appeared in her life. He wasn't without faults. Of course he had faults. Who the hell didn't? He could be a little bad-tempered, he could be a bit stuck in some of his ways too. But, Lord God, how happy she was to have found him. Happy? No. It was much more than that. If she hadn't met this man, now, she would probably have been alone for the rest of her life. She knew that. Robert was a kind man and a real man, and she had met him at the last possible moment. Perhaps there was a God, after all.

The music stopped. And Robert turned to her.

Lori smiled at him. And Robert smiled back. A handsomely crooked smile, his eyes sparkling.

"Put it on again", said Lori. "I know you want to".

Robert laughed.

And Lori smiled again.

"No", he said. "Something for you instead".

Lori drew long on the joint then blew out a huge cloud of blue smoke. "That slow Beyoncé track".

Robert nodded. And as the sky, through the long narrow window began to turn dark, Beyoncé sang the slow version of 'Crazy in love'. Robert set the track to loop. And he came over to Lori, who was lying stretched out on the mattress. He sat beside her.

It wasn't a bed. Not a proper bed. Just a huge mattress, positioned on the floor, near to the window, and covered with cream duvets and a beautiful Chinese blanket, woollen and multi-coloured. The window was partially open and street sounds came in, but nothing intruded. Joss sticks burned and the room smelled sweet and fresh at the same time.

Not only had they found each other, quite late in life, but together they had re-created the whole feeling of being just 20 years old. Every morning would be a lie-in, if Robert's work allowed that. A lie-in until whatever time felt good. And it was OK to be dressed or undressed, play music or talk about art. A deliberate, and successfully deliberate, attempt to recreate a carefree period from earlier in life. His student days. Her 20s. And it worked wonderfully well.

Lori passed the joint to Robert. And the sea-shell ashtray, too. He didn't smoke any of the joint, just held both things for Lori.

Evening was drawing in. And the two of them were topless. Lori's long, long legs were bare too. Robert was wearing jeans.

Yes, from even a short distance, they would have looked like a couple in their 20s too. They had each kept their shape, kept their love of life. And that, in itself, given what both of them had experienced, was a little miracle.

"I grew up feeling like a girl. It was that simple. And for me it was the most natural thing in the world".

When lovers first find each other, their stories must be told. Without them, without those stories, there can be no real bond, no real friendship. Nothing worthwhile.

And the only time to tell such stories was before, during or after the most intimate moments when everything else in the world ceased to exist or, at least, ceased to matter.

This was one of those intimate moments.

"When I was four years old, all of my friends were girls. All of them. I thought nothing of that. Of course I didn't. We hadn't started school yet and we were just little girls growing up in a tiny village in the Cotswolds".

"How tiny?" asked Robert.

"Really small", Lori replied, not turning to look up at Robert's face, just needing to talk. "There were only a dozen or so houses.

And the only other children in the village, at least the only other ones the same age as me, were girls. And those, all of them I think, were my friends".

Outside a dog barked, just once. And the sky darkened a little more. Blue turning turquoise.

Robert, still holding the joint and the odd ashtray, lay down next to Lori.

"One day, about October I suppose it must have been, because we were all talking about Christmas presents, one girl, Angela, who was probably my best friend at the time, said that she was going to ask for a Barbie doll. My other friends wanted Barbies too. And so did I.

"I'll never forget that day. We were sitting on the wall of the churchyard, the three of us, and then it was time to go in. Two of my friends went home one way, but me and Angela went the same way. Walking and talking without any cares. We got to my home and my mother was there. She was outside, in the garden, talking to one of our neighbours. Angela stopped, and this was what I said to my mum, and I remember it as clearly as if it was yesterday. I said 'Mummy, for Christmas, can I have a Barbie doll?'

"It was a horrible moment. Because my mother turned to me and, in a really nasty voice, which I'd never ever heard before, said 'No. Don't be stupid. Of course you can't have a doll'.

"I was really upset. I didn't understand. I didn't understand at all why my mum was so cross with me, and I didn't understand why I couldn't have a doll.

"'But Mummy', I said, 'Angela is getting a Barbie doll. Everyone is. Why can't I have one?'"

Lori turned to look at Robert. He was lying on his back, taking care of the joint, watching the ceiling as if it was the only thing in the world. Lori reached for the joint and Robert felt the movement. He passed it to her. But not the seashell ash-tray; that was placed on Robert's chest.

"Our neighbour, who I'd never liked, because she was always saying odd things to me and seemed to watch me all the time, said 'You can't have a doll because you're a boy. And boys don't have dolls. Only girls have dolls'. Then she laughed. A horrible laugh.

"I suppose, for a few seconds, I probably didn't know what to do or say. But then I burst into tears and ran indoors.

"A little while passed, and I was in my bedroom crying. I mean really sobbing. Then my mum came in, and she was crying too. She took hold of me, and held me, and told me she was so sorry for speaking to me like that. She explained that she loved me and promised me she would never speak to me like that again. I asked her if I could have the Barbie doll. She said no. Dolls were only for people like Angela and the others. For girls. And she used the same words that our neighbour had used; she told me I couldn't have a doll because I was a boy".

The last of the joint was smoked, the ash flicked carefully into the seashell and then Robert took the cigarette from Lori's slim fingers and stubbed it out.

He rose, without speaking, and chose another quiet piece of music.

"That's awful", he said softly, meaning it with all his heart.

Lori nodded. "That was the first time in my life I realised I wasn't the same as my friends. I felt so sad. And even when my mum made me a cup of warm milk, and told me a bedtime story, after she'd gone, I cried and cried and cried. And from then on, it had all changed. Although I tried to play with my friends the same way, it just didn't feel the same. Not any more. And when they all got dolls for Christmas, I didn't want to play with them. I had soldiers instead. Plastic soldiers".

Robert came back to Lori's side and stroked a loop of her ice blonde hair away from her big green eyes.

"Did you ever get that doll?" he asked.

Lori shook her head. "No. From then on my parents seemed to make a deliberate effort to make me feel like a boy. Plastic guns, a football kit and football boots. Then more soldiers. And I even ended up with about seven or eight footballs. But I didn't want any of that. And, as time went by, I learned that there were toys my parents would let me have, which were gender neutral. So I had toys like plastic farmyard animals. And my Dad thought that was because I wanted to become a farmer. One of our uncles lived nearby, and he was a farmer. And so I could play with those animals. And, really, they were my new friends, so to speak, because ever since that experience with the Barbie doll, I had felt alone.

"From then on my parents kept me like that too. Away from my friends, away from girls. But that wasn't out of spite, or anything like that – they did it because they loved me. In their own way, confused and wrong, yes, but they thought it was right. They kept me indoors, mainly".

Robert sighed and shook his head slightly. What was there to say? Often dealing with rough types, in the building trade, he thought he had seen and heard it all. But this, all of this, his new woman, her story... it truly shocked and saddened him.

Robert had been through a lot himself. Growing up on a tough council estate, he had quite literally seen his brother killed in a motorbike accident and watched his mother become an alcoholic and then die from the disease. But all of that was now years ago. And since then he had gone on to set up and run his own business and now, today, he even employed a dozen men and took time off almost at will.

"What happened when you started school?" he said at last. "Did things change then?"

"Yes", Lori hesitated. "But also no".

Robert nodded. And the dog outside the window barked again, as if to announce the arrival of the bright moon which had just appeared above the roof of the neighbouring house.

The moon shone with a deep yellow colour – the tone it always seemed to adopt when the air was warm and the next few days promised sunshine.

And for a while, close to each other but not touching, they lay and watched that moon as it began to pass slowly across their space. Listened to soft music. Listened, even, to the hushed sounds of a big city at night.

"Were you allowed out late?" asked Robert at last.

"No", said Lori, her voice little more than a whisper, not wanting to disturb the calm gentle night.

"I was always out late", said Robert, also quietly. "Always in trouble".

"When I started at secondary school, the boys there picked on me. I was thin and pale and blonde and nothing at all like any of them. I just wanted to play with the girls", said Lori quietly.

Robert turned towards her and studied her face. Lori had been a model. As a 'male'. And she was stunning, whatever her gender. And maybe the fading light also took away some of the years, too. Was this how she had looked in her 20s?

"My parents took me to see a psychologist", said Lori, turning on the mattress to face Robert, her back now towards the window. "He told them I was a girl and they were horrified. My mother said 'No. I brought a son into this world. Not a girl. He can be gay, but he cannot be a girl. No. I will not have that'".

Robert sighed.

Lori raised herself up on her elbow, small but beautifully formed and wholly natural breasts pointing towards the mattress.

"That was how it was", she said. "How it's always been, really. Being transgender, people think it's a joke or not real or whatever. But I was born like this. There was a problem with my sex when I was born, ectopia, and I was given all kinds of crazy, contrasting medicines, everything. I was a boy but also a girl. But me, I grew up knowing myself to be a girl. Inside, the real me, that was only ever a girl".

"I know, babe", said Robert gently. "I know". He brushed away that same lock of blonde hair, which had fallen once again across her big green eyes, tucking it gently behind one of her ears.

Lori lay back down on the mattress, stared at the ceiling for a moment, then edged closer to Robert and laid her head on his chest, her hand lightly stroking his strong arms as she did so.

"People think transgender is just something weird, kinky. Perverted. Something all about sex". Lori spoke quietly, almost to herself. "It isn't that. For some people it might be, I don't know. But for most it isn't. I was born like this. And then society treats you like you're some sort of specimen in a test tube. It laughs. It points at you. Men see us as a fantasy. Women push us away and call us men. For most of us it's a life full of suffering and pain. And abuse and suicide or self-harm".

Robert reached for Lori's face. Lifted her chin up, so that her eyes crossed slightly as she focussed on his face. He leaned slightly towards her. And then kissed her gently on the lips.

Lori smiled, almost purred, and laid her head on his chest once again.

"I thought I was a monster", said Lori quietly, without turning to face Robert.

For a moment, perhaps because of the calm of the evening, and the slow but ineluctable approach of sleep, reality seemed distant and Robert wasn't sure what Lori meant. So he simply nodded and said, "In a dream, you mean?"

But Lori shook her head a little. "No. No. When I was little. I thought I was a monster. Abnormal. An alien even."

Sleep retreated. Robert stroked Lori's hair. "When you were little?" Of course he couldn't understand it all. Not fully. How could he? But that wasn't important. What *was* important was that he was on her side, really, finally, for once – he was a man who was on her side. He would try to give her whatever she wanted. Needed. And now, in the small hours of that morning, what she needed was just someone to listen to her.

"Yes", said Lori, "For years, that went on for years. I didn't want to make my parents suffer, I didn't want to be different, difficult. So I was an androgynous teen dressed in asexual clothes. But inside I was sure that I was some sort of monster. It wasn't really until I arrived in London, and mixed with gays, because I hoped I was gay too, that all that began to change".

"They helped?" asked Robert.

"Yes", said Lori, lifting her head slightly, turning towards Robert's face. "In some ways. They told me I wasn't a monster. And through them I learned all about transgender.

"That was such a relief for me. After years feeling I was alone and some sort of horrible... *thing*.

"But then the anger... All that time blaming myself. The anger I felt when I realised that I wasn't a monster, that was horrible too".

Outside the window, a blackbird was now singing.

"It's late for that", said Robert quietly. It *was* late for a blackbird to sing. The sky was darkening now, very much so.

"Perhaps something's disturbed it", said Lori.

"Or perhaps it's been a very long way from home and only just got back", said Robert.

At first Lori didn't respond. She lay with her head on Robert's chest and her hand was still. Then she spoke. Just one word. "Home".

And then, for a short while, the two of them slept.

When they had first met, Lori had decided to tell Robert everything. To be totally honest with this man.

And there had been a lot to tell.

For Lori, the problem wasn't just finding a man who accepted her, it was also about telling that man all about the chaos which had been – in so many respects – her life up to that point.

To have found such a man meant everything to her.

Everything.

No wonder the single word 'Home' now felt sufficient.

Except for the faint glow of a small and dim orange lamp, it was dark when Robert woke.

The window was still open but no smoke curled upwards any longer from a joss stick.

Lori – as she could – had already risen and moved away as silently and as carefully as a cat creeping up on a mouse. The quiet hours of the morning were not a time where Lori found rest.

Robert guessed that she was in the bathroom. Already, several times during their relationship, Robert had woken to find Lori elsewhere, usually asleep on a sofa but sometimes not even that, perhaps in the bathroom, alone, and smoking a joint.

Silent to avoid disturbing Robert. Silent and often disturbed within. Unreachable at such moments, she would half sit, half stand by the window, watching the trees weave and dodge in the wind, watching rain fall or, as tonight, just watching the stars, still and calm in a dark blue sky.

Robert lay unmoving for a moment and then got up, still wearing jeans. He was annoyed with himself because he had fallen asleep with those on, and the bed must have got too warm for Lori.

The music, too, had long since stopped. Or perhaps Lori had stopped it when she woke. He didn't know. So he found some more ambient tracks. The sound of waves on a beach, the distant sound of thunder, those kind of things. Relaxing. And he pressed play.

And with that, he took off his jeans and climbed under the thinnest of the duvets, setting aside the Chinese blanket. It was mild, without being warm. There was no need for a heavy cover.

He lay and listened to the waves, almost falling asleep. But also waiting for Lori.

Then Lori re-appeared, now naked.

She turned off the pale orange lamp and reached for the duvet.

The room was now lit only by distant streetlights and the night itself. Shadows and darkness in which only silhouettes and a few details could be seen.

"Oh no", said Robert, laughing quietly. "No you don't. I want you to stand just where you are. Let me look at you".

Lori smiled. A huge smile. She had once been a model and she wasn't remotely fazed by nudity – nor by posing. So she pretended to pose. And Robert laughed. She did it again. Then wrinkled her nose and stuck her tongue out.

Robert scanned her from top to toe. The long lean body. The shadows. Angles. Curves. The tousled bleach blonde hair – which wasn't, in fact, bleached, but was naturally an almost white blonde.

"Let me in", said Lori at last.

Robert pulled the cover back, and Lori climbed in beside him.

"You feel gorgeous", he said. "Cool. Soft. Just wonderful".

Lori kissed him. Just once. Just lightly on the cheek.

And once more, they adopted their favourite position. Robert lay on his back and Lori rested her head on his chest as he put his arm around her.

With gentle music playing, a very slight breeze blew in from the open window. And for a few minutes the two of them said nothing. Did nothing.

And then, slowly, faces turning towards one another, they began to make love.

Robert's kisses were gentle. Lori's were even gentler.

There was time enough to be kind, to show warmth for one another.

Different tracks now played, still the soft breeze blew and their kisses slowly became more passionate.

For Robert, every previous partner had been born a woman. Lori had also been born a woman, but it had taken over 40 years to correct her sex to match her true gender. When they had first met, naturally enough, Lori had been worried about that. About how Robert would react.

In fact Robert told her, the very first time, that he adored her. That he found her sexier than any other woman. And this evening, once more, for a long lingering time, he ran his tongue in and around her, Lori clutching at the pillows as he did so.

"At last", she moaned, when he finally changed focus, "I have a real man".

Intercourse itself required the man to be patient. To understand and to control himself more than ever before. Because Lori couldn't easily be taken, sex had to be gentle and lubricant had to be used. Smiles and soft words – these mattered almost as much as physical contact. But none of that reduced the enjoyment. In fact, for Robert, that patient build up increased the enjoyment. With Lori, it wasn't just sex, it was really about making love. About sharing. And for Lori, too, it worked to have a man who respected her like that.

Time passed. Another cigarette was lit. Smoked slowly.

Robert laughed and touched Lori gently on her naked shoulder. "I really don't need to know. It really doesn't matter".

Lori, sitting up now, legs under the thin duvet, blew out a big cloud of smoke and nodded. "I know. But I want to tell you.

Because it does matter". Then she turned to look at Robert. "But you must promise to try to understand".

"Lori", said Robert sincerely. "I will understand. Whatever it is, it's fine. I'm not a judge, I'm your partner. Your man".

Lori nodded. It was hard to relate what she had to tell. But it had to be done. It was, really, the one thing she had yet to discuss. The one major part of her past that she hadn't yet told Robert about. And she knew that honesty was the only way forward. But she was scared about how he would react.

"Altogether", she began slowly, "it must be, probably, close to two hundred. And it could be more".

Robert didn't flinch.

Lori turned, in the half light, and studied his face.

No. There was nothing. Not the slightest change of expression.

In fact Robert shrugged. That was all. He just shrugged. "There", he said, leaning forward and kissing Lori gently on her shoulder, "It's said. And I told you, it doesn't make any difference at all".

"Thank you", said Lori. "I mean that. Thank you".

The night outside was now silent. And inside, too, the ambient music had finished. It was quiet, the only noise being the faint snoring of the cat. Robert's cat. A cat Robert had found and rescued. It was happy and healthy, but it would always have a chest problem because of being abandoned and abused as a kitten.

Lori smiled at the sound. So did Robert.

And, as she finished her joint, the two of them lay back on the mattress, her head once more finding his chest.

"It began as soon as I arrived in London", said Lori.

Robert put a finger to her lips. "It's OK", he said. "Really it is. You don't need to say".

Lori hesitated. Didn't move. "I know", she said at last. "But I want to".

And with that she resumed her story.

At the age of 18, Lori had not been wholly female. It had been another 20 years or so before her sex realignment surgery had been completed. And for much of that time, a great deal of life had been hell. As simple as that, really – it had been sheer hell. Nevertheless, arriving in London as a teenager, she had been picked up on her first night out by a man in his early 50s. A day or so later, he took her to a hotel. A day or two after that, he promised to 'look after her'.

"What did that mean?" asked Robert quietly.

"He seemed nice at first. But he wanted to install me in a flat. Keep me as his mistress. Pay for everything. He was one of the most senior police officers in the city. Married, with children at the best schools. And he wanted this, me, a beautiful blonde transgender trophy. And I was the same age as one of his children".

And so they talked.

About how one man after another, after another, had been overwhelmed by this transgender fantasy. But none of them, not one, had wanted a genuine – and public – relationship.

She told Robert all this. And he just accepted it. What shocked him was the degree and extent to which ordinary men seemed to have the desire to sleep with a transgender woman, yet never form that real relationship.

Had she wanted, Lori assured Robert, she could have slept with dozens of men, every night of the year, every year, and never met the same man twice. And almost all of them, she told him, would have been married with children and in higher end jobs.

That was the fetish. The fantasy. The thing which so very very men longed for. All the more so, in Lori's case, because she was naturally so attractive and feminine. Stunning.

Men, she told David, had even ejaculated just by looking at her.

Eventually, in understandable despair, Lori had thought about killing herself.

At that time, just a few years previously, her life had reached that nadir.

Some of this was said with smiles and laughter. It all seemed so ridiculous, so distant, like scenes taken from a bawdy erotic tale. But also, of course, some of it was incredibly difficult to say and to hear.

"So... you mean you've never had a proper relationship?" asked Robert quietly, still finding that, of all things, the hardest part to believe. Lori was gorgeous – inside and out. How could she not have had a partner?

Lori shook her head. "No, never. I wanted that more than anything but it just wasn't possible. There's such a barrier. If you meet someone you like, and they like you, there's the usual attraction... All the time I know, at some point, I have to say, 'Oh, and by the way, I have a penis'. How do you tell someone that? When?"

"You did try".

"Yes!"

"It was bad".

"Yes. Very bad. Once or twice men reacted calmly, even nicely... then disappeared. But I've been punched. I've had drinks thrown at me. A man who thought, one moment, that I was a beautiful woman, a man who seemed so gentle, suddenly he would hit me or hurt me.

"Men wanted me because I was a beautiful girl with something extra. Taboo. Exciting. But every time I heard 'dirty tranny' in the street, I couldn't even get out of bed for a week".

"Jesus Christ", said Robert. And with that he held Lori a little closer.

"It wasn't just men, though", said Lori. "I mean that rejection. It wasn't just relationships, it was everywhere. Sometimes I've been to see a doctor with just an ordinary problem, but I've been turned away and told 'we don't want *your sort* in here'. I've had to work all my life without telling most of my colleagues the truth".

"They think you're a woman".

"I am a woman!" said Lori.

"I know, baby, I know", said Robert. "I mean, it must affect the things you can do, and share".

Lori nodded. "Once, from work, everyone wanted to go swimming. I couldn't do it... You can imagine".

Robert laughed. A small laugh.

"What?" asked Lori.

"You", said Robert. "Like that. In a swimsuit. Having to hide parts of yourself".

Lori pinched Robert. Just slightly. Playfully.

"Ouch".

"You deserve that", she said.

"Sorry", said Robert, smiling. "I'm sorry. That must have been awful".

Lori lay her head back on his chest.

"It was", she said. "It first happened to me at school.

"Swimming?" asked Robert. "God. To think how much I hated that. And that was just because I couldn't swim".

"Swimming costumes. Oh, it was horrible. I was 11 years old, dressed as a boy, and made to join the boys for stuff like gym. Then I started to develop breasts. I told my parents and they took me to a doctor. I was prescribed strong male growth hormones. Injections. That stopped my breasts developing further but it didn't turn me into a boy.

"I finally got a letter to excuse me from gym on health grounds. But that was after I'd been made to go swimming a few times. It was awful. Just horrible".

Robert had no words.

"I know", began Lori slowly, "That now, all these years later, I can talk about it. And it seems somehow distant. Almost as if I'm just telling a story about someone else. But in here..." she tapped her head, "I can still see so much of it".

Suddenly there was an extra weight on the mattress. Re-homed stray cat or not, Fitch was no longer a little lightweight. And when he decided to jump onto the bed, his weight was unmissable.

"Oh, Fitch", said Robert. "You want something?"

Fitch brushed his long tail in Lori's face and then did the same with Robert.

"I'll get him a few crunchies", said Robert, climbing naked out of bed.

Robert was gone for about ten minutes.

And during that time, deep in thought as she often was, Lori rolled another joint, lit it and smoked it.

Not more than once or twice, during that whole time, did her huge green eyes blink.

They reflected. They shone. But they didn't blink.

"Why didn't..." began Robert as he got back into bed. "I mean, didn't anyone give you counselling? Did your parents sort anything like that out?"

Lori waited until Robert was lying down. Then she resumed her favourite position. She laid her head on his chest. And as he stroked her white blonde hair from her face, she told him something he hadn't expected to hear.

"There was nothing", she said quietly. "No counselling. Nothing. I don't know if that was because my parents were ashamed and wanted to hide me, hoping it would all somehow go away, or maybe there was just nothing available. People had even less idea back then, about transgender and so on, than they do now. So I just went through it all feeling like that monster or freak I told you about. I didn't even know if there was anyone else like me. Not in the whole world".

Lori hesitated. Chewed briefly on her lip. Wanting to find something happier to think about. To say.

"At school", she said, "because my parents, especially my mother, wanted me to be a boy, I had to ask other boys what to do".

"What do you mean?"

"Well, I was small and very feminine and some of the bigger boys, for whatever reason, sort of stood up for me. And became very friendly. Not sexually, I mean. Nothing like that. They just looked after me. And one of them, a huge blonde boy, became my best friend at school. He played rugby and all the girls liked him".

"So what did you do?" asked Robert, a smile in his tone.

"I told him my secret", Lori replied. She lifted her eyes towards Robert. And smiled. "And from then on, whenever I didn't know what a boy was supposed to do or say or behave like, in a given situation, I asked him and he told me".

Robert laughed.

How wonderful.

That in all that awful hurt and pain, such kind people and such considerate moments could be found.

"Maybe the world has some hope after all", said Robert.

Lori moved.

It was time to sleep.

She lay next to Robert now.

Each with their head on a separate pillow. But still touching, gently, softly, from time to time. Letting fingers speak. Connecting to one another without words.

And for a time, that was enough.

Without ever realising it, Robert had spent his whole life looking for a woman such as Lori.

And Lori, very much aware of it, had spent most of her lifetime looking for a man who accepted her as the woman she truly was.

Lori sighed. Heavily.

And sleep began to return.

*

Two months later, the relationship broke down.

The relationship both had spent their whole lives waiting for.

Robert came home from work one day, and Lori had left him a letter. Ten pages long. An outpouring of hopes and dreams and then, at the end, some only half clear reasons as to why she had gone. A long lonely afternoon under a grey November sky had taken its toll on her. On both of them. On everything they were and everything they could have been.

Immediately? Losing Lori felt colossal. Tears, pain, loss. Those came. Hugely. Robert hurt.

But why? Why had she really gone? That question arose and stood towering above all others.

It made no difference how often he read those ten pages. There was always a gap between the bulk of her letter and her abrupt and hugely sad conclusion.

She had waited all her life for him. Why had she gone?

Robert wasn't perfect. He knew that. But who was? Surely it was about finding the person who came closest to that for us? In her letters, she wrote about how he was kind, capable, handsome and stylish, she saw that he accepted her gender totally, that he could be the most gentle of lovers and the most thoughtful of men. But wasn't he also, at times, too brusque, too tired, too down on life? And through that, she felt, too hard on Lori?

Yes. Yes he was. He was all of those things. He knew it.

He had never raised a hand to Lori – he never would – but he had, on a few occasions, found himself tired out and dour, moody and unable to light up Lori's world the way he wanted to.

Maybe that was, in part, because Robert was Scottish. There is an immensely capable and practical side to the Scot, but at times that crosses into the unhealthily frank.

More likely, much more likely, it was the fact that, for all her pain, all her years of suffering, abuse and sexual self-abuse, Robert, too, had known hard times. Sometimes very hard. And those had left scars inside, which sometimes manifested themselves in outward signs. Being down on life. Robert felt, at times, that he had also spent years in the trenches. Undergoing every kind of siege. Seeing his best friends die, others too. Because sadly, is a real part of everyone's life. For men too.

It seemed to him that, for dozens of her own reasons, Lori hadn't been able to see any of that. Not really.

If Robert raised his voice, her fears took her back, back before Robert, to other men who had assaulted her.

If Robert felt his fifty odd years, and seemed sometimes set in his opinions, that took Lori back, again before Robert, to countless other men who had harshly ordered her around.

Something that was nothing at all, really, just small things which called for her gentle persuasion, a delicate touch, a kind word, to Lori had become "fear of abuse and assault".

And Lori, clearly, had felt that she was better off away from that.

But there was more to it, and Robert knew it.

The answer wasn't in the letter.

Did Lori have depression? Yes she did. To some extent.

Robert knew that.

Depression is still very much misunderstood. It isn't just about darkness or suicide; depression is also about a whole host of other emotions. Distrust, panic and fear, for example. Those, too, are key to depression. Emotions and feelings which don't necessarily show themselves as we might expect – but which are all too real. Depression kills but it also destroys. It undermines, it eats away like a cancer.

That Lori, after so many years of pain, abuse and even sexual self-abuse suffered from depression – that was understandable. In truth, given what she had gone through, it was almost a miracle she was still alive, and not just alive but coping and trying hard to live a normal life. She was brave, she fought, but at times things simply got too much. And that, in truth, was what had happened with Robert.

Was depression the cause of the break-up then? No.

The reality was even simpler. As reality often is.

Two people, who may have spent forever trying to find one another, can drift apart for the wrong reasons. By accident, they can reach a situation which is then irretrievable. It is no one's fault. Life can be a bastard like that.

Lori had once said she could no longer love.

And, in all her tangled words, half-truths, moments and glances, searching to find a way to be, Robert knew that was the real reason she had left.

She didn't love Robert.

Or, rather, she didn't love him *enough*.

And he knew that was the truth, because he felt exactly the same. Two tired people in their fifties cannot love easily or fully. If they are to find love, it may well take years. A short-term passion will pass. Love, real love, a tender bond forged over time, for all the small mistakes and faults made en route, will last forever.

Robert felt that way about Lori. Saw and knew that this was a relationship which could only take years to build. He was ready for that.

But Lori – that youthful internal part of Lori – still believed in miracles.

And she had gone, moved away, probably in search of one.

And for all Robert looked, as time passed – and he did look – and for all he sought out his woman, he would never find her trail and never discover that Lori had moved, albeit in stages, to the south coast and to Brighton. Suffering, en route, one or two more genuinely bad relationships and sinking, slowly but remorselessly into a chronic – and potentially deadly – depression.

Wasim's story

On the estate where I grew up, we were very lucky. For some reason or other the council, or whoever was responsible for these things, had left long fingers of grassland, wild grassland, untouched, that reached right in from the countryside along the river valley. Right into our estate. The heart of the city.

We spent hours, every hour, especially in summer, playing by that river. All sorts of games. We sailed sticks, built dams of mud and played hide and seek in the long grass. But we had more than that, we also had a stately home nearby, disused and spooky, and running up to it a long splendid avenue of trees, oaks and horse chestnut. Yet more grassland. So if we didn't want to play by the river, we played football or cricket on the grass, in that avenue of trees.

On top of all that there were parks. Municipal parks with slides, bowling greens, climbing frames and even a wooden maze that we all loved. A cafe which opened erratically and sold four sweets for one penny.

Yes, we were lucky. The city was huge and sprawling and to have all of that green space was rare.

Of course all the children I grew up with lived on that estate too. The same estate. So I'd never met anyone of my own age from any other sort of background. But that changed at secondary school where, suddenly, there were boys and girls from further out, out in the countryside – though not very many of them – and there were also boys and girls – very many more – who came from deeper within the concrete tangle of urban space.

One of these was Wasim, the first Pakistani boy I'd ever met.

At first, to our eyes, white, Western and poor, Wasim seemed strange. Different. There were black kids at our new school too, but they appeared confident, intimidating to us, and we all very quickly learned to keep out of their way. But Wasim was the only 'brown' child and we didn't know what to make of him.

On the one hand, Wasim was small, but he laughed all the time and that made him appear bigger somehow. Larger than life. He spoke very quickly, too. And it took some weeks before we could understand him. If the teachers asked him to read out loud, they would often tell him to stop after just paragraph or two – because they couldn't understand him either. So he was different and we could have felt intimidated by him. But we weren't. Because, on the other hand, Wasim didn't take part in any sports. Why? We didn't know. But that was strange. Real boys liked football, so why didn't he?

There were other lessons too, that he seemed to avoid. And he never sat through the prayers in assembly. We didn't understand any of that. But nor did we care. When he wasn't laughing, Wasim was incredibly self-effacing, almost disappearing from view. And so I think all of us, more or less, quickly forgot he was there.

And that was how things were until the beginning of the fourth year. We led our lives at school, and he led his.

Then it all changed.

The city centre, which we all called 'Town', was a long bus journey away from our estate. As part of that journey, a journey we all knew so well, the number 55 bus passed through a dark part of the city. Coronation Street – it all looked like Coronation Street.

Row after row of red brick Victorian houses stood like tired soldiers waiting to be pensioned off. Old narrow streets that had surely seen better days. Tiny terraces, front doors opening directly onto traffic-filled roads, exhaust fumes rather than fresh air, and at the back of each, nothing more than an alleyway for a garden. Dilapidated shop fronts, one in particular a miserable bottle green, with dirty soot stained windows.

This part of the city was somewhere we were very glad not to live. There were no avenues of trees here, no long fingers of grassland, no river valley. And as we sat upstairs on the bus, passing through those narrow crowded streets, occasionally seeing children kicking a ball about in dark narrow roads, we felt, if not better than them, certainly luckier than them.

Where we had privet hedges, they had curb stones. Where we sat on grass verges, these people sat on those curb stones, in the gutters of their narrow streets.

Of course such children, these children, all of them, were just like Wasim. They were 'brown' too. They must have been the same as him and so they must have been different to us. There was a sort of logic to our thinking. Their clothes, their mannerisms and, presumably, their families and their homes. All different. Not that we cared. It was an innocent prejudice. But we saw all those differences.

Yet on that day, going 'up Town' on the bus, for some reason my friends and I were surprised to see Wasim walking along these same dark streets.

Why were we surprised? Despite – or perhaps because of – having been at the same school now for four years, we had never associated Wasim with this desperately poor area of the city. Yet, at that time, things were ghettoised in exactly that way. There were areas of the city for white people, areas for black people and areas for brown people. It wasn't an exclusive arrangement, not legally enforced, but it was more or less the way things were.

"There's Wasim", said my friend, Kevin, very suddenly. "What's he doing here?"

We stood and craned our necks to see him. To try and see what he *was* doing. But he disappeared into a shop before we could work it out.

"Come on", I said, "Let's go and see".

And so we got off the bus. Three of us. Kevin, Tony and me – Neil.

Even though, by now, we were 14, nearly 15 years old, I'm sure that for all three of us this was the first time we had ever got off the bus in those dark narrow streets, so filled as they were with things vibrant, strange, fascinating and seemingly different.

"Which shop did he go in?" asked Tony.

We weren't sure.

"That one, I think", I said, pointing to a small shop window filled with the most wonderfully coloured assortment of materials I'd ever seen.

"It's a dress shop!" laughed Tony. "I'm not going in there".

Kevin and I agreed. And so we waited outside, the air choking with traffic fumes just as I had always imagined it must be in this narrow place.

Suddenly the door of the shop opened and Wasim appeared carrying three or four large plastic bags, filled with what seemed to be red, yellow and green silk. Though actually none of us, us three, knew the difference between nylon and silk.

Then Wasim saw us.

The moment could have been difficult.

But Wasim just smiled, one of those huge smiles he had always been so ready to produce, and any awkwardness immediately passed.

"What are you doing here?" he asked in that voice that had once seemed so odd to us but now felt wholly familiar.

What were we doing there? For a moment we didn't know what to say.

"We were going to town on the bus and then we saw you", said Kevin.

"What have you got there?" asked Tony.

I almost said 'Do you really live around here?', but I was glad that Tony's question had prevented me from asking such a thing.

"Material. It is my sister's wedding, and I am collecting some material for her to make clothes".

Tony nodded. And for another moment, we didn't know what to say.

"So what are you going to do with it now?" I asked, rather awkwardly. It was a daft question. I knew what the answer would be even before Wasim replied.

"I'm gonna take it home", he laughed. "You think I'm gonna walk around wearing it?"

I laughed too. So did Kevin and Tony.

And with that, Wasim began to walk.

Where? Home, we guessed. And we instinctively tagged along with him.

Very quickly we turned off the main road, the one the bus travelled along, the one we knew so well from behind those often grubby bus windows, and entered into a long rambling street that looked totally alien to us.

Later I would see the same streets in Lowry paintings. But that was many years later.

We walked along with Wasim, in this new world, ours the only pale skin visible in each street we passed.

The pavement was too narrow for the four of us. So I walked next to Wasim. And Kevin and Tony walked just behind.

Eventually we turned into a very narrow cul-de-sac; there was no road here, just houses, facing directly into each other's windows. Close enough, almost, to reach from one home to another, across the cul-de-sac and shake hands with a neighbour opposite.

Really it was quite horrible, cramped and dark. But it would have been impolite to say as much.

"Listen", said Wasim stopping. "I live in the end house".

The three of us looked at the end house. It had a bright yellow door. The brightest yellow we had ever seen.

"But you mustn't come any further".

Kevin fidgeted uncomfortably.

"Why not?" asked Tony. "Can't we come in and have a cup of tea?"

Wasim shook his head. "No. My father, my mother too, and my brothers, they are quite strict. Not like me".

I nodded. "It's OK", I said. "It doesn't matter".

"Oh, but it is not so serious", Wasim added, excusing himself or his family, I wasn't sure which. But – I now realised – it was an expression he often used.

We exchanged a few more words, then trudged away again.

I didn't know how Tony or Kevin saw things, but I knew that I couldn't imagine growing up in such confined spaces.

And, at that moment, I think, I felt a sense of respect, or something like that, for Wasim. For the fact that he came to school and smiled all the time, while he lived in such an impoverished place.

Yes, that was where our friendship began. And that was why. It began with that feeling of respect.

*

Two years later, Kevin, Tony, and most of the other faces I had known for the last five years, had left school. They had taken their 'O' levels, and now they were either at work or unemployed. I had wanted to leave school as well, but the headmaster had insisted that I stay on to take 'A' levels with a view to going on to university.

There were perhaps no more than 20 of us who had stayed on. Most of those were girls, but Wasim was one of the other boys.

Sixth formers, which we all now were, led a fairly relaxed and unstructured life at school. We rarely used any of the classrooms where younger pupils were taught and where we ourselves had spent five years, and instead almost all of our time was now spent in a small modern annex informally known as 'the huts'. They were not huts. There was nothing garden shed like about them. But they did feel rather detached from the main school buildings. Almost as if we were being educated in someone's garden.

The day would start with a very informal registration period. It was not at all unusual for one or two students to arrive as late as 10 am, long after registration had ended. Lessons often proceeded in a similarly informal manner. The teacher might sit on the desk, or two lessons might more or less merge into one another. I wasn't studying French, but on several occasions my art history A-level overlapped with the French group and I found myself listening to art history in French.

In short, being in the sixth form was easy-going. And that was quite intentional. We were moving on, growing up, learning to form new friendships.

Only a month or so into this new order, I began to see a side of Wasim that, for some reason, I had never expected. It just wasn't the kind of thing we thought about. Not back then.

Wasim had developed a close friendship with several of the girls, and I saw that he did so without any of the embarrassment or difficulty so familiar to all boys.

He was very comfortable with them. And they acted with him almost as if he was a brother. There was no sign of anxiety, no flirting, nothing like that.

One afternoon, rocking precariously back on my chair as I waited for our politics teacher to arrive, I leant towards Wasim and asked him how he managed to be seemingly so cool with the girls. One in particular, a girl called Karen, had been – and still was – the best looking girl in the school. I was delighted she had remained on into the sixth form, but with her I still found myself tongue-tied. So how did he do it?

Wasim smiled. Still that big smile. Always there.

"I am gay", he said. As matter of fact as that. "They know it. So I feel very much at ease with them, and they feel comfortable with me".

I hardly knew what the word 'gay' meant. Vaguely, yes. In detail, no. But I nodded all the same.

From then on Wasim and I often talked about girls, and about being gay. And, in all honesty, I enjoyed talking to Wasim more than I cared about any of the lessons. Going to school meant learning from my Pakistani friend.

It wasn't long, however, before the subject of boyfriends arose.

Did he have a boyfriend, then?

No.

Had he had one before?

No.

Why not?

And this was where he told me a little more about his background, his family, and about being a Muslim. And as he talked, I recalled quite vividly that bright yellow front door.

"Of course I love my family and they are good people. But they are also strict Muslims and it would be impossible for me to tell them that I am gay. They do not know. They talk already about marriage and weddings, children and grandchildren. I play along because I do not want to hurt their feelings".

It all sounded rather strange to me. If Wasim was gay, then he was gay. There was no point disguising the fact. It wouldn't go away. I was also surprised to hear that some parents could be so strict. My own were very open about everything. And so, just like when I'd compared that river valley, those long green fingers of grass where we played as children, to the streets where Wasim had grown up, I suddenly felt very lucky. Privileged almost.

"What will you do?" I asked him later, as we left 'the huts' at the end of the day.

He smiled, "I do not know", he said. "I will have to wait and see".

We said goodbye, and he walked off. To catch a bus back to those little dark narrow streets and that happy front door.

I watched him go.

He seemed very small to me at that moment. But then he *was* quite small. Much smaller than me.

For the next few weeks, Wasim wasn't at school.

It was coming towards winter, perhaps he had a cold. Certainly the teachers seemed unconcerned. When Karen commented on his absence, they simply said, "He will be able to catch up with the work".

But when he finally did appear again, I could see straight away that something was – or, rather, something had been – wrong.

We didn't get the chance to talk properly until lunch time.

"Where've you been?" I asked him. "You've missed tons of work".

Wasim's reply was non-committal. And I didn't want to push him, so I changed the subject. "Hey, guess what?" I said, dying to tell him my news. "I'm going out with Karen!"

For the first time that day, Wasim's face lit up. That same old smile. The one I had seen so very often.

"How did you manage that?" he asked me.

I told him the truth. Karen had actually asked me out. Not the other way around.

Wasim laughed.

The final lesson of that day was free. So I decided to go home early. Normally, Wasim had Physics during this time. So I was surprised to see him come into 'the huts'.

"Are you going home early?" he asked me.

I nodded.

Wasim shook his head. "I must tell you", he said. And with that, he sat down.

There was no one else in the room. I wasn't in any rush, so I sat down too.

"I told my parents", he said.

For a brief moment I didn't understand.

"I told my parents that I am gay", he said with a little more force, realising that I hadn't understood.

"Oh", I said. "Wow. I see".

I wasn't sure what to say. Was that why he had been missing from school? I didn't know.

"Erm... so, what did they say?" I finally managed to ask.

Wasim glanced down at the floor. It was very quiet in the room for a moment. "They were very angry", was all he said.

What that meant exactly, I had no idea.

Suddenly Wasim looked up at me, the big smile returning to his face. "It is not so serious" he said. "It's not".

I felt that those words were forced. I felt that his smile was forced too. But I didn't want to press the matter. So for a while we changed the subject and talked about lessons, homework, university and my first date with Karen.

Then it was time to go home.

As I walked home, a 30 minute walk along that green river valley of mine, I wondered why Wasim had been off school. Had something bad happened as a result of his telling his parents that he was gay? Or had he been off school for a wholly different reason?

I didn't know.

18 months later, the mock exams had been and gone. The real 'A' levels were almost upon us.

My relationship with Karen had been and gone too. But Wasim and I were still friends.

Both of us were now 18. Both ready to leave school and, hopefully, go to university. We talked often – and intimately – about relationships.

I had had several.

Wasim had had none.

"University will be very different", I said. And I meant it too. For, surely, once free of his family and their strict attitudes towards gays, Wasim – who was good looking, intelligent and always such a positive person – would have no problems at all in finding the freedom to have a relationship.

Generally, when we talked like that, Wasim agreed with me.

He was very much looking forward to university. More than most, I imagined. And for good reason too.

But sometimes, and today was one of those times, he seemed low.

That was understandable.

Family meant everything to him, I knew that, he'd told me so many times. But so too did the fact that he was gay. He was gay and that was that. He had as much right to find happiness as the next person. But the clash, that clash between family and love, at times, I saw it clearly, it could get him down.

I remembered the first time I had taken a girl home – my Mom had been so happy to meet her. My Dad too, I suppose, in his own more or less indifferent manner.

To be unable to do that... Worse, to actually offend and upset your parents by doing that... it felt like a dreadful thing to me. And, not for the first time, I was glad to be poor and white and free of any such worries. I didn't envy Wasim his situation.

"If I do ever meet a boy", he said, "I will never be able to take him home. I hate that".

What could I say?

We talked. The mood passed. But I knew that the pressure was there. I knew that his happy, outgoing nature would only cope with so much.

Sure enough the exams arrived and, probably because of that extra pressure, Wasim did have a brief breakdown.

A good student, with good grades, and certain to go to university, he missed his first exam completely. He just didn't turn up.

Everyone was shocked.

We soon found out, however, that he was in hospital. He had taken a whole bottle of aspirins.

Even in the middle of my own exams, I had to go and see him. And so I did.

I visited Wasim in hospital and called him a stupid this, that and the other.

"Don't be so crazy", I told him. "Things will work out. There's always an answer".

Sitting up and looking surprisingly well, he laughed. Admitted he was stupid. Said that it was the pressure of the exams.

"And don't tell me that this isn't serious", I said. He laughed again and said that he wouldn't.

We talked a little longer.

He said that he wouldn't be allowed home for another three days.

"Oh. So what will happen about your exams?" I asked. He would miss the next one too, because that was due tomorrow.

But, apparently, all of that had already been sorted. The school was fine, in his case, with him sitting the missing exams at a later date.

In fact, as it turned out, Wasim did not sit any of his 'A' levels that year.

The school was supportive and flexible, and he was allowed to take that whole year again.

"There is one good thing", he said to me, when we met at a bus stop, and quite by accident, a few weeks later. "By sitting through all the coursework a second time, I will be sure to pass my exams with flying colours!"

And so I left school and went to university.

Wasim fell behind.

And we lost touch.

*

It was the very early 1990s, and I was attending my third or fourth rave when Wasim and I met again. Quite by chance.

Life can be like that. School is particularly bad. Relationships can be formed, and they may endure for five years but, on the day we leave school, they are often lost for good. It isn't anyone's fault, it isn't deliberate, but it happens all the same and it happens often. There's something wrong in there. Bringing people together, often from great distances, only to let them fall apart. Were humans meant to live that way?

The rave itself was in the city centre. Town. Others had been in stately homes, out in the countryside. Long queues of cars, meeting at a motorway service station and then driving, following the people who knew, for some distance to a secret venue.

I loved them.

Everyone loved them.

There was no alcohol. There were no hard drugs. And people from all walks of life, all ages, mixed and danced and smiled.

That, anyway, had been my experience out in the countryside.

Perhaps here, in the big city, in the inner city, things wouldn't be so easy going.

That uncertainty made for extra tension. And, in one way, that tension also made for a better night. For me, when things were too predictable, too uniform and too happy, they became boring.

The venue for this party was a disused municipal building. A great vast cathedral-like place built, unusually for this city, out of red sandstone. Gothic or neo-gothic or something in that style. It had towers with ornate windows and halls with high ceilings. And in the middle of the building, in the very centre, there was a huge hall flanked by balconies.

I had visited the building once before, many years ago, as a child, to buy books from a special educational event. Back then the building had smelt of Jeyes fluid and varnish. Tonight, already, it smelt of people and cigarettes.

The interior was dark. Pitch black. Or, to be accurate, it would have been pitch black but for the dozen or more neon tubes and strobe lights that flickered and flashed, illuminating colourful hangings, suspended from the balconies and anything else which could be reached.

I looked up, already dancing, as the place began to fill. I couldn't see people on those balconies. Not clearly anyway. Just the tops of heads. Could hear laughter and voices.

The night was fun. And it would go on, and on, until maybe 7 am or even a little later.

Dancing, however, even revved up with a small tablet of ecstasy, was tiring. At least from time to time, I wanted to stop and take a break and wander around and look at people.

Ecstasy did that. It made you want to look and experience. It made you want to talk to strangers. And laugh. Share the whole event. And they, invariably, would talk and laugh back.

During one of those breaks, with only a bottle of water to drink, I wandered through labyrinthine passages and corridors until I found myself on one of those balconies above the great sprawling dance floor.

For a while I stood and watched. Wide-eyed. Quite literally wide-eyed.

I had come to the rave with some friends, but where they were right now, I didn't know and it just didn't matter. Like me, no doubt, they were in here and out there at one and the same time.

It was fine. All of it was just fine. The world felt good.

I'd already said hello to dozens of strangers, and hugged quite a few too. So it was wholly normal when an Asian lad about my age came up to me with a big smile and threw his arms around me.

"Neil!" he shouted. "How are you?"

"Fine", I smiled.

We hugged.

And then I realised who it was.

This was no stranger; this was my old schoolmate, Wasim.

"Waz?" I asked, stepping back and half-peering at his face.

He grinned, white teeth brilliant in the light from UV lamps, his white T shirt dazzlingly so.

"How are you?" he asked again.

And we hugged each other once more.

And then we both began talking at the same time. Excitedly.

We were both well.

I now had a master's degree. Did he ever get to university?

Yes he had.

We talked about that.

Then, from the dustier recesses of my memory, came that question: 'Did you have a boyfriend? At university, I mean. Did you ever get that boyfriend?'

No. That didn't happen.

I wondered, as we spoke about it, if he was still gay. As if being gay was a condition. Something that could get 'better' or 'worse'. It was the early 1990s – we meant well but we didn't necessarily understand.

Happily, Wasim must have guessed what was going on in my mind because he answered the question I hadn't asked.

"Yes", he said. "I am still gay and I do have a boyfriend *now.*"

"You do?"

"Yes!" Being gay, he told me, wasn't a fashion.

I laughed. That reply made me feel good. A boyfriend. So, somehow he had found his way, then. I was glad of that.

By now we were both back down on the main dance floor. And dancing. The music flowed, we spoke, separated, came back together. Spoke some more.

Perhaps five minutes passed like that. Perhaps it was two hours. I had no idea and I didn't care. I knew it felt good to see Wasim. He looked fit and happy. But then I guess I looked fit and happy too.

"Good to see you again", I said. Probably for the tenth or twelfth time.

Wasim laughed. And I laughed too.

Lights flashed. Impressions swam. Figures came and went.

"What about your family?" I asked him, as we stood in the chill-out room a little later, drinking only water and surrounded by countless people doing the same.

He shook his head. Clearly that was not so good.

I changed the subject. "Hey, guess who I'm seeing now? Karen. From school. Remember?"

He remembered. And we laughed about that, too.

But the subject of family came back again.

This time Wasim looked a little down. Understandably so.

"I've still never told them", he said. "I want to but I can't".

I nodded. Try as I might, I had no idea what that must have felt like. We were in our late 20s now. Would soon be 30-something.

"Where do you live?" Wasim asked me.

I told him. It was a very leafy suburb. Full of flats and students and people who made music.

"And you?"

He told me. It was also a suburb full of flats. But it was dark and dangerous. Half of the streets were red light.

Suddenly old thoughts came to my mind. There I was, today, again, living in a nice green area, big houses now, but green and leafy once more. And there was my friend, small and smiling, still living in dark narrow streets. And I still didn't envy him.

That was wrong wasn't it? He was intelligent, positive and kind. Why wasn't he in a nice suburb too? I sighed.

A few more hours passed, the rave ended, and we went – we all went – back to our homes.

But from then on, for a while – because life has a habit of doing things like this – I saw Wasim quite often.

I bumped into him in the city centre. Town.

I bumped into him in a suburban high street.

We were at another rave together.

And then, one dark and wet night, in the rougher part of the city, the part in which Wasim still lived, we bumped into each other in a backstreet pub.

Wasim was himself. As ever. Smiling.

But the boy he was with – his partner – was surly and diffident.

And I knew why. His partner was taking drugs, but not the kind that made you happy or the kind that made you talk. This was the other kind. The kind that took you, slowly but surely, down.

Wasim disappeared for a while. An hour or so. Then we met again at the bar. I bought myself a beer and him an orange juice.

"What's he using?" I asked, going straight to the point.

Wasim wrinkled his nose.

It was smack.

That meant trouble sooner and later.

I told Wasim. But he already knew it.

"He promised me he'd give it up".

I nodded. "Do you think he will?" I asked.

Wasim smiled. "It's not so serious", he said.

*

After that, I didn't see Wasim again for quite a while.

Not at any of the raves, which began, in any case, to become mainstream. And that meant alcohol, bouncers, fights... all the usual stuff.

Nor at any of the 'usual' shops in town.

Nor in any of the local pubs.

I even made a point of going to that same back street pub, on several occasions, even when there was no real reason for me to be there.

But I didn't see him.

All those years earlier, I had been travelling from my poor estate to the city centre on a bus, with friends from school, when, suddenly, we had looked down and seen Wasim.

And that was how I finally found him again.

The same bus. The same route, going home from a Sunday lunch with my parents, who still lived on the big estate where I'd grown up.

Reading a book, to alleviate the tedium of the bus journey, at one point – probably in the same street as all those years earlier – I looked up by chance and there, crossing the road, was Wasim.

I didn't hesitate. I jumped up and rang the bell and the bus came to a stop within a few seconds. I got off the bus and, at first, I couldn't see my friend.

Instinctively, I suppose, I headed off down a side street, somehow expecting him to be there.

And there he was. A hundred metres ahead of me. A thin looking plastic bag in his hand.

"Waz!" I shouted.

At first he didn't turn, didn't respond. So I shouted again.

"Waz!"

He stopped. Turned. Saw me and, yes, as ever, he gave me that huge smile.

I caught up with him. We hugged.

"Every time I see you", I said. "You seem to get smaller!"

He smiled.

We both smiled.

"What are you doing here?" he asked.

I explained my day, my book, my bus. "And you?" I asked. "Are you still seeing that same guy?"

Wasim shook his head. "No. He wouldn't give up the drugs".

An elderly lady coughed, and we half turned and realised we were blocking the narrow pavement.

I stepped into the road.

She thanked me and continued on her way.

"So you're single again?" I said.

Yes.

"I'm sorry", I said.

I wanted to say something, to ask about his partner, to show that I was there for him, somehow, but I couldn't find the right words. So, instead, I asked him once more about his family. A family I felt I had known for many years, but never once met.

Wasim shook his head. "No. It is much worse now. I argued with my boyfriend about the drugs, we had a terrible row. He followed me back here and my family found out about us. It was horrible".

There was more. I knew it. So I waited.

"They have told me that I must now leave the area. Leave the city for good. If I don't leave, they will beat me up".

"Oh my God." I couldn't help my words. "That's insane. Just insane."

Wasim nodded.

I wanted to ask him when all this had happened, but that felt too personal.

"So", I began, "So... what are you going to do? I mean, what are you doing now?"

Wasim lifted the thin plastic bag, just slightly.

"I have just been to my home. There were a few things I wanted to collect. But they refused to let me in, and my brother came out and told me to go or he would hit me. He said that I was making my father ill".

Fucking hell.

Then a thought occurred to me. If I had taken time to reflect, it would surely have seemed a wholly inappropriate thing to ask, but I didn't reflect, so I asked it anyway. "So... what's in the bag?"

He shrugged. I understood. And for a moment neither of us spoke.

In the background, children began kicking a football around in one of the all too narrow streets.

"What are you going to do?" I asked at last. "Where are you going to go?"

"Brighton", Wasim replied without hesitation. "I have a distant cousin down there".

Paul's story

The school bell rang and Paul wasn't in his seat. In fact he wasn't even in the classroom and that meant only one thing – trouble.

Men were wearing platform shoes and flared trousers made of nylon. In a few years' time, the Sex Pistols and punk rock would make their first appearance. The 1960s were a thing of the past, the summer of love long since over, but in schools – even mixed underfunded comprehensive schools in the large cities – discipline was both still strict and strictly enforced. Being late for class, at the very least, meant detention. Perhaps even the cane.

Paul, however, was only vaguely aware of those rules, because this was his first day at secondary school. Term had begun six weeks earlier, but Paul had been unable to start school at the same time as all the other new boys and girls. And as he limped heavily along the corridor, it was visually very clear as to why that had been the case.

Paul had been born with an ailment that had disfigured his left leg, and it had taken several painful operations, carried out in stages over six or seven years, to repair most of the damage. The most recent operation – and the one which had kept Paul out of school – had more or less resolved the condition, but Paul still limped and he would continue to limp for some years to come. Though, of course, he was unaware of this on the day he found himself late for school.

For any child, starting a new school can be a daunting experience, but at least if everyone starts at the same time that fear – and that excitement, too – is shared. After all, even some of the teachers are nervous. But to arrive so many weeks after the rest, and to do so with an all-too-visible problem, was asking for trouble.

Form room doors were made of heavy wood, foreboding and stern, with only a very small rectangular glass window set at head height. Paul finally reached the door of his new classroom and hesitated before opening it, his face framed in the little window, portrait like.

Inside the classroom, every head turned, including that of the teacher.

The term was still relatively new, but pupils had quickly become accustomed to faces briefly appearing in that small window, prior to the door suddenly being opened. Usually, of course, the person who then entered the room would be a teacher, often the black cloaked Miss Harrison, deputy head of the lower school and feared, or so it appeared, by staff and pupils in equal measure. Occasionally, however, a girl or a boy already known to the others would arrive late to brief jeers from his or her fellow classmates.

Paul didn't fit into either of those categories. And to make things worse, his hesitation, his being framed in the window, allowed those jeers to begin in earnest even before the poor boy had opened the door.

The teacher, already bad tempered that day, and annoyed by this sudden outburst of noise, glanced up and realised that there was a boy outside peering in.

He strode across to the door and flung it open at the very moment that Paul had applied his weight to the handle.

Needless to say, Paul more or less tumbled into the classroom, crutches and boy clattering against the desk nearest to the door.

The room erupted with laughter.

The teacher, red-faced and embarrassed by his own mistake snapped at Paul.

And the girl whose desk had been displaced by the stumbling boy took the opportunity to pick up one of the crutches and lean on it.

"Long John Silver", said the girl sitting next to her.

"Peg Leg", a boy shouted from the back of the class.

The teacher, of course, quickly took control of the situation. But he did so at Paul's expense.

"The bell went 10 minutes ago", he said. "Where have you been?"

"Detention!" said a chorus of voices. Laughter.

"The whack", said another. More laughter.

"I... I..." stammered Paul, not having any idea how to explain how or why he had arrived late.

"He's hopped all the way here", shouted one boy.

"Peg Leg", said that same voice again.

Finally, the teacher did assert his authority, telling the others to be quiet, and suggesting to Paul that he sit down at the remaining empty desk. A desk, unlike all of the others, alone. At the front of the class with nothing to look at except for a pale blue wall with flaking paint.

It had not been an auspicious start, and at break time – his first break time – needless to say, things got very much worse.

Stephen Betts was very much the form bully. Stephen's had been the voice shouting "Peg Leg", and it had been Stephen who, during Physics, the first lesson of the day, had told the others,

"Don't sit by Peg Leg, because you'll catch a disease". School, certainly inner-city school, could be like that. Red hair, glasses, being overweight, being tall, even being intelligent, all of these and more were things which marked you out and made you some sort of a target.

But it wasn't until break time that Stephen Betts paid any more attention to Paul.

"Why are you on crutches?" asked Stephen, as several of the boys stood in a small group around the coffee machine.

The real answer? Because life can be bloody unfair.

But Paul had no answer. At least, not one that made any sense to Stephen. Neither the name of the condition, nor any sort of explanation that this wasn't a contagious disease, meant a damned thing to Stephen Betts. And so the bullying began in earnest.

"Give me your money", said Stephen.

One of his cronies, a scared little blonde boy called Andrew Marshall, pushed Paul against the wall and Paul – in part because of his condition, in part because he was frightened – wet himself. Not a lot, but enough for the other boys to notice.

There were shouts, screams and laughter, all in equal measure, and Paul, shaking, handed over a few coins to Andrew.

Andrew passed the coins to Stephen, but Stephen threw them on the floor.

"I don't want that!" he snapped. "Not after he's pissed all over them!"

Andrew laughed.

Other boys laughed too.

Then Stephen shouted, "Come on, let's get away from him, he's dirty".

"He's a leper", said Andrew. They had learned about leprosy in History only a few days beforehand.

And the boys scattered, laughing.

For a few minutes afterwards, Paul struggled to collect his money. First with both crutches under one arm, and then laying the crutches down as he reached under a bench for the last few coins.

Home life, of course, was very different.

Perhaps too different.

And when Paul came home from his first day at secondary school – catching a specially arranged taxi that made him stand out even more in the eyes of the other children – and his parents asked him how it had been, he told them it had been fine.

In other words, he lied.

That wasn't because there were any problems at home. There weren't. Not in the normal sense of the phrase 'problems at home'. But because Paul had been affected, since birth, by his condition, his parents had taken a lot of time and trouble to make sure that he had always been supervised, protected... cossetted, even.

His parents had meant to do the right thing by him. They were both good, honest, hard-working and loving people. But affection, when it becomes too protective, can be as harmful as anything else. Children need to experience a few bumps and bruises without being fussed over. A cough isn't always whooping cough. A sneeze isn't always an early sign of pneumonia.

There were two other children, as well, neither of whom had the same condition. They were very nice. And they, too, overprotected Paul. Always placing themselves between him and any trouble.

And yet, in turn, they also felt some deep seated, slight but real resentment at the extra care and attention Paul always received.

So when Paul came home from school, having been bullied all day, he didn't want anyone to fuss over him. Nor did he want his brother and sister to feel neglected. Because even at such young ages, children are always aware – however vaguely – of such things.

Nor did he want his parents to rush up to the school the next day and make a fuss about what had happened. Because he felt that such a visit would only make things worse.

And, of course, he was right.

Unfortunately, as is the way with such things, and as the bullying continued over the next few weeks, the truth did finally come out. And Paul's parents were both horrified and sympathetic towards him. They were horrified that he had been bullied, but understood that he hadn't wanted to tell them.

"Please don't come up to school", said Paul, as his mother insisted on tucking him into his bed.

"We'll have to say something", said his Mother. "We can't just leave things to go on".

The following day, after dropping Paul off at school, Paul's father went and spoke to the headmaster. And a few hours later, as the form assembled for afternoon registration, the face of the stern Miss Harrison was briefly framed in the little window in the heavy wooden door before she entered, without knocking, and interrupted the form teacher.

Stephen Betts was to go with her, immediately.

No one knew what for.

And a short while later, Stephen Betts was proudly showing off the marks of the cane, on his hands, and boasting about being given a week's worth of detention.

In a way, the cane and the other punishments, only served to increase Stephen's standing as a bully to be reckoned with. But that didn't prevent Stephen from, very publicly, threatening Paul with being beaten up for having grassed him up.

"You're dead, Peg Leg. After school, I'm going to have you".

Of course, after school, Paul was taken home by the specially arranged taxi. And so Stephen Betts didn't have the opportunity to carry out his threat. But that opportunity did arrive just a few days later, whilst everyone queued up, outside the woodwork block, waiting for the always late Mr. Jones.

The woodwork block, built some years after the main part of the school, was situated right next to a pond – the school pond, in effect.

It wasn't deep. But it did have a muddy bottom and was partially filled with weeds.

And as the boys queued up, they often fooled around right on the edge of the water.

By now, Paul was friends with a couple of boys in the school band. They both played cornets and were adamant that Paul should also join the band and learn to play an instrument.

And they were talking to Paul about the types of instruments available, when Stephen Betts and his crony Andrew Marshall and a few others came over to Paul and started to push him around.

"You got me the whack, Peg Leg", said Stephen.

Paul tried to move away, but Andrew prevented him from doing so.

"Why can't you leave him alone?" asked Robin, one of Paul's new friends.

But neither Stephen nor any of the others paid attention. Instead, Stephen snatched one of Paul's crutches, and began doing Long John Silver impersonations.

And the crowd of boys grew and laughed.

At first, as Stephen did this, Paul felt uneasy. He felt, as he had done since the operation, that he could neither stand nor walk without his crutches.

But in fact that wasn't true.

And as Stephen performed all the more, right on the edge of the pond, Paul realised that he could now stand without any aid. More than that, he also realised he didn't feel afraid of Stephen Betts any more.

"Give me my crutch back", said Paul, with a surprisingly confident voice, one born perhaps of many years of pain and suffering which other boys of his age hadn't yet known.

"Make me", laughed Stephen. And then, turning nastier in tone, "Come on, make me".

Paul took one slightly hesitant step towards Stephen.

And Stephen took one step towards Paul.

"Peg Leg", said Stephen, now immediately in front of Paul.

"Have him!" said Andrew. Meaning for Stephen to hit or kick Paul.

Paul half turned to look at Andrew, then turned back fully to face Stephen Betts. And then he hit him – Paul hit the bully – squarely on the chest.

Stephen, still half-resting on the crutch, staggered, twisted and fell into the school pond.

Totally. Not just feet or legs, but a full-length tumble.

There was uproar.

Laughter and shouting.

Paul recovered his crutch. And Stephen, still in the water, stood up. Soaked head to toe and covered in weeds and mud.

If the story had ended there, it probably would have been a very good thing.

But Paul was angry now. All those years of pain. And from somewhere deep inside him, came a rage – albeit briefly – that he was unable to explain later.

As anyone who has ever used a crutch for any length of time will know, arms get stronger and stronger the more you use them. And Paul had much more strength in his arms than he could possibly have realised.

And as Stephen Betts tried to clamber out of the pond, Paul swung the crutch at him with a good deal of force, hitting Stephen on the side of the head.

There was a horrid crunching noise.

And Stephen fell back into the water.

Mr. Jones, their teacher, finally approaching from the staff room, saw only the tail end of things. And no matter who else said what, Paul was in trouble again.

Stephen Betts died.

There was plenty of support for Paul. The death had been a horrible accident. The provocation extreme and proven. Officially, apart from being sent to a different school, 'for his own good', there was no further punishment.

Sadly, rather than the change of school being the end of the matter for Paul, his parents, brother and sister, this was only the beginning.

Six months more passed and his parents felt the pressure to move not only home, but jobs and city too.

So Paul moved to a third school.

Perhaps it was that move, the upheaval of his family, the tearful arguments involving his brother and sister, who didn't want to move, so close to their exams, that changed Paul from being a kind and positive boy into a surly and difficult one.

Or perhaps, as some said, there was always a strange and inexplicable anger inside him.

Whichever it was, from that point on, Paul was always in trouble. And things went from bad to worse.

*

Paul left school at the age of 16. That was a huge disappointment for his parents; they knew, they were sure, that he could do better. He ought to have stayed on to do 'A' levels. He ought to have gone to university.

Paul left school at the age of 16. That was also a huge relief to his for his parents. Paul's time at school had been nothing but trouble. Detentions, work not being done, bad reports, even some fights.

Both of those viewpoints were felt. Both were true.

In addition, Paul's mother and father were now living in separate homes. Separate cities.

His mother had gone back to Bristol, their original home city. She lived there now with Paul's brother and sister, both at the university.

His father had remained in Manchester, with Paul, who had joined a local engineering company as an apprentice.

An engineering apprenticeship lasted for four years. And for the first of those years, dozens of boys – because they were almost all of them boys – were based in a technical college in the east of the city.

The main building of the technical college was a great draughty Victorian property, divided up into high-ceilinged classrooms. Lessons in metallurgy, technical drawing, mathematics and suchlike.

Behind that building, lay a large courtyard filled with sprawling, low-rise industrial units, each specially built for the teaching and learning of various engineering skills.

One long low shed, dark and which always smelt strongly of sulphur, was used for welding. Boys, becoming engineers, were taught how to braise, using brass, and weld with blinding electric arcs.

Another even longer, lower, darker shed, was used for sheet metal work. How to bend and fold metal to create a huge variety of useful items such as toolboxes and protective guards.

And then there was the main workshop itself. Built in the 1960s, with a flat roof, illuminated with strip after strip of fluorescent lighting, this building was where the apprentices learned how to use lathes, milling machines, a forge and, of course, hand tools of all kinds, sizes and shapes.

Here, weeks were spent using a hacksaw to cut a perfectly straight line in an unforgiving lump of metal. If the line went off course, it was time to start all over again.

Yet more weeks were spent filing, endlessly filing, to achieve a smooth and precise curve on a metal bar. A horrible task that would have depressed a saint. But one that, it had to be said, taught the boys that anything, and everything, was ultimately possible. And perhaps, really, that was the point of the chore?

Paul made friends easily and quickly at college.

In part that was because he was intelligent, quick-witted and good looking. But in part that was also because, periodically, he did the most crazy and even the most dangerous of things.

Needless to say, it was one of those that soon landed him in trouble and lost Paul his place as an apprentice.

"What are you doing?" asked Paul one afternoon, having grown bored of trying to saw a straight line in metal.

Barney – though that wasn't his real name, just a nickname – was a great cricket fan. "We're re-playing the one day game against Australia", he laughed.

The main workshop was large enough to hide in, as long as that hiding was done with a gentle sort of care. There were big machines, milling machines and lathes in particular, which created a kind of dead zone. A space where the instructors couldn't see the apprentices. Not easily. And not without being seen approaching.

Paul stood for a moment and watched.

Barney had unscrewed a hard plastic knob from the controls of a lathe. And that knob had become a makeshift cricket ball.

He then rolled it, along a workbench, to Mark. Mark, with a hammer in his hands, was the batsman.

"Who's winning?" asked Paul.

"I am. Australia", laughed Mark. "Currently 150 for the loss of only four wickets".

Paul watched.

Barney rolled the 'ball' along the workbench. Mark nudged the thing off the edge with the hammer and that, apparently, meant four more runs added to the score.

Paul watched a little longer. Another boundary. Four more runs.

"It's too easy", said Paul. "No wonder England are losing. Bowl properly".

Barney laughed. "OK", he said.

And with that, he bounced – gently, that gentle care required to avoid discovery – the ball down the workbench.

Mark laughed. And he softly pushed the ball back to Barney.

And Paul edged closer, wanting to join in.

With bounces and hitting, rather than rolling and pushing, the game had suddenly taken on a louder and slightly more risqué edge.

Mark looked up, to see if any instructors were aware of the game.

Barney did the same.

"Next ball", said Paul. Encouraging, but not yet taking an active part in the game.

Once more Barney checked if any instructors were watching.

They weren't.

He bounced the ball, low, slow, just once, in the direction of Mark.

Mark knocked the ball back down and along the floor.

It rattled as it rolled along the concrete floor. Hard plastic noises.

"We'd better stop", said Barney, worried that the game was getting too much, too obvious.

Mark nodded.

It had just been a daft way to waste ten minutes. The cricket season was on. They had been talking about the game. And then, harmlessly, they had played a little game of their own.

"No", said Paul. "Don't stop. Give me the ball".

Barney did so. A mistake.

"You go and stand by the door", Paul said to Mark. "That can be the wicket".

Mark laughed.

Just a few metres away, there was a half-glazed door, which led to a rarely used office.

"I'll bowl", said Paul.

And he walked perhaps five metres or so away from Mark.

Then Paul turned, jogged towards Mark, mimicking the run up of a cricketer, and bowled the hard plastic knob with a degree of force.

The noise of the hard plastic 'ball' bouncing in the workshop was altogether too audible.

And rather than strike it, Mark sensibly caught it, laughing. "That's enough", he said. "Gripes is looking over. We'd better put the knob back on the lathe".

And Mark tried to do just that.

But Paul wouldn't let him.

"No", said Paul. "I want a go now. It's my turn to bat".

"Gripes is looking", said Barney.

"Just one", said Paul, determined to have a go. "Just bowl me one".

Mark looked round. Gripes – Mr. Gripley – was no longer visible. That probably meant he was coming over to see what the noise was.

"OK", said Mark. "Just one. Quickly".

And taking just a few steps away from Paul, Mark gently lobbed the hard plastic knob in the direction of the 'batsman'.

Paul, presumably, forgot where he was.

He swung the hammer as if it were a real cricket bat. As if there were a good hundred yards to a white boundary rope. He swung the hammer and made a very strong and clear contact with the 'ball'.

Crack.

The hard plastic knob flew through the air.

Straight over the head of the instructor they all called Gripes.

It flew like a bullet.

Bouncing once or twice as it landed, each time with a very loud clacking sound. It hit a lathe, probably still travelling faster than a car, and ricocheted off in a wholly random direction.

But that wasn't all.

The hammer – or at least the metal head of the hammer – also flew through the air. Paul hadn't let go of it – it had simply come away from its handle.

It too landed with a crash, turning over a metal tray full of oil as it did so.

Everyone saw.

Everyone heard.

It was dangerous, stupid and it wasn't going to be forgiven in a training college dedicated to safety first, safety second and safety third.

Paul was expelled from the college. He had been warned before about doing stupid things. But this was considered a step too far. Someone could have been seriously hurt.

And with that expulsion, he was also dismissed by his employer and lost his apprenticeship.

As with Stephen Betts, some said that Paul had been badly and wrongly treated. What had happened wasn't his fault. And even if he was to blame, in some way, his childhood had been so difficult, in very many ways, because of his illness. He clearly needed some sort of care or help.

Others thought that Paul *was* to blame. That he was 'wrong in the head'. Yes, maybe that was down to the drugs and medications he'd had to take as a child, but whatever the cause, the blame lay at Paul's door and no one else's. He was dangerous, wild, unpredictable.

*

The appointment was for 9 am and Paul wasn't there. In fact he wasn't even in the building and that meant only one thing – trouble.

Women were wearing dreadlocks and combat boots, and for the last few years Ecstasy had been the drug of choice for pretty much everyone under the age of 50. It brought all sorts of people together – young and old, black and white, gay or straight. Sure it had some tragic stories – but nothing compared to the legal killers like tobacco and alcohol. Raves were commonplace, jobs were once again plentiful and things, for most, were looking up.

But there were still many people for whom life seemed only ever to take a backwards, downwards step. And Paul was one of them.

147

Since losing his apprenticeship, leaving home at the age of 20, joining and then leaving the army, falling into and out of one job after another, one home after another, one relationship after another, Paul was now on the fringe of the dance music and underground scene, and even there he wasn't really wanted.

But today, he was meant to be signing on. More importantly, today he was meant to be at an interview to check that he was still 'actively seeking work'.

And he was late for that interview.

Under pressure from the chaos of the early 1990s recession, the government had decided to allow the unemployed to sign on just once every eight weeks.

That was sensible and it was generous. It worked, too. It gave the administration time to catch up on the enormous backlog of work. And it created – or helped create – a much less tense situation at places such as the unemployment benefits office. Not so long before, there had been bulletproof screens, long waiting times, harsh tannoys and security staff. None of that had made things any better. When the screens were removed, the staff encouraged to chat with the job-seekers, music played and so forth... the atmosphere improved and attacks and abuse disappeared. But rules were still rules.

"I'm afraid you've missed your appointment, Mr. Evans", said the girl at the reception desk. "And I don't think we can fit you in today".

Paul was annoyed.

He had taken a bus, in plenty of time, and of all days for it to happen, the bus had bumped up off the road, over the curb and crunched into a parked car. The police had arrived before anyone had left the scene and asked everyone to wait and give a statement.

Paul was one of those.

But the whole explanation sounded ridiculous even as he told the receptionist why he was late.

"Will I lose my benefit?" he said.

The girl shrugged. She just didn't know.

"But I *am* here", said Paul. "It wasn't my fault".

"But you've missed your appointment", said the girl.

And the conversation went around in circles for ten minutes.

Slowly but surely a queue formed up behind Paul. And he was politely asked to move away. He did so. But he remained in the Job Centre, trying at several opportunities to see someone about the situation.

Finally Paul was told to go home for the day. Nothing more could be done. He would hear a decision as soon as possible by letter.

Two days later, the letter arrived.

Regretfully... you failed to attend... Benefits suspended for six months... right to appeal... etc. etc.

The short of it was this: Paul had no money. Nothing. And that included housing benefit.

He had been in a few tight situations before, but this time it felt wrong, cruel. He went to the police station and asked for some sort of proof regarding his statement. There was nothing they could do.

"But I had to make a statement", he said.

The desk sergeant agreed. But the statement was involved in a legal dispute. It couldn't be released.

"But I missed my interview because of that. And now they've stopped my benefits. I'm going to lose my flat too!"

Would the police communicate with the employment service and sort it out?

No, they would not.

Paul lost his flat. And from there, he found himself sleeping on different floors in different homes – and he began to steal.

It wasn't the first time he had stolen.

He'd lost his last but one job for doing exactly that.

He had stolen some petty cash from his employer.

And that had gone onto his record. And no one with a CV that stated "Fired for theft" would find a job easily.

So here he was again. Nowhere fixed to live and no income.

But this time there was a difference. This time he was on the periphery of a circle of people who used acid techno and Ecstasy to have a good time.

Drugs were easy to find.

And it soon became apparent to Paul that stealing someone's drugs was more profitable than stealing some cash.

And so that was what he began doing.

At first it was Ecstasy and the odd bag of mushrooms or similar. A few speed tablets. But then, finding himself in a squat – at the very bottom end of the system – where heroin was the escape of choice, he began stealing that, too. Not using it. Just stealing it to sell.

And, with that, stealing itself became a habit.

Anything valuable.

Any time.

Very quickly Paul had more money than before. Much more than he got from signing on. And quite a bit more than he had earned from working.

What was the point in doing either when both brought in less than stealing?

At times, yes, he was found out. But Paul was strong now. And he had learned to look after himself. And if things did become too heavy, he simply moved to another squat.

Time passed.

Months became years.

Finally ostracised by the students and DJs, the urban travellers and artists, Paul moved further away. The city was big. There were lots of places to hide. Paul knew, saw and understood that he could have gone on running and stealing almost indefinitely. Until, in one tower block, sleeping on the floor of a casual acquaintance, something happened that brought an abrupt end to this easy but tragic and broken existence.

The tower block wasn't the sort of place where peaceful nights or sleep arrived easily. If Flat 576 wasn't playing loud drum n bass, then Flat 578 was having a loud screaming argument. If both of those flats were quiet, an alarm in Flat 580 was screeching, remorselessly, pointlessly, until it exhausted itself five days later.

Doors were forced open almost as often as they were unlocked. There was nothing unusual about seeing a mattress, in flames, falling nine or ten floors to the dog-shit covered, tyre worn grass below.

It was that kind of estate.

And on this particular night, dark and cold, maybe two dozen people had come back for a few drinks and a few smokes.

"I know you, don't I?" asked a friend of the acquaintance. A man seated in one of the few chairs.

Paul, who was sitting on the floor, drinking from a tin of lager and smoking a joint, didn't recognise the face. And even if he had done, he wouldn't have blindly owned up to it. The friend of the acquaintance could be anyone.

"We were at school together", continued the friend, whose name was Chris.

Paul shook his head.

Chris leaned forward. "We were. You were on crutches. Then you left".

Paul blew out some smoke and took a longer look at Chris.

Was this man the same age as Paul? Paul would be 40 soon. This man looked too young. "I don't think so", he said at last.

Chris nodded. "Yeah, yeah, we were. There was a right nasty kid there called Betts, I don't remember his first name. Everyone hated him. And you brained him one day with your crutch!"

Paul looked again at Chris. And nodded. Still reluctant to commit.

"He died didn't he?"

Paul shrugged. It was all so very long ago.

Chris sat back in his chair, a brief flash of solid gold bracelets as he did so. Paul's eyes couldn't help taking those in. They were huge and these last few years of peddling anything stolen he could get his hands on had taught him what was, and what was not, fake. Those bracelets were solid gold. Expensive.

"Yeah, that's right", said Paul, thinking about the gold. "I don't remember you, though."

Chris shrugged. "I was just a little shy kid back then. I'd been bullied a lot before you rocked up on those crutches". Chris gave Paul a strange look. As if, somehow, sussing him out. "I owe you a favour for getting rid of Betts".

Paul nodded.

For a moment neither spoke. Then Chris seemed to be considering something. Then he leaned forward and spoke quietly to Paul.

"I'm guessing, looking at you, that you aren't exactly flush at the moment?"

Paul shrugged. "I do OK", he lied.

Chris shook his head.

Paul looked at him again. The clothes Chris wore were out of place in this dump. It was those, and his sun tan, that made him look younger than Paul. And money too. No doubt of that. He had money. He ate well. All of it. All of the things Paul and so many others didn't do, Chris did.

And of course, Chris didn't let it go at that. He wasn't the sort of man who let things go. He had done very well for himself. And he had done so by selling large quantities of hard drugs.

He wasn't one of the faceless men who owned hotels and private jets. Nor was he one of the men who, more or less, ran the gangs controlling drugs and prostitutes in the big cities. But with close ties to the right people, and a personality that others always took to, he was now in a position where money would never be a problem again.

And so, an hour or two later, sitting in the back of a car being driven by someone else, Chris and Paul were laughing about the old days.

Memories of their school.

Not that Paul had very many memories of that school. But that didn't seem to bother Chris.

"Listen", said Chris as the car stopped at a set of red traffic lights. "I'll do you a big favour, Paul. And, if you handle it properly, I think we can help each other".

The lights changed and the car started up. It drove 50 more metres, then took a left turn down a dark lane and stopped, now on the edge of the city centre.

Chris glanced out of the window. There was a dark and heavy looking door there. Painted black. It appeared to be a very strong door. The rear of a nightclub. It had that sort of feel.

"Come here, tomorrow", said Chris. "Ring the bell. Tell them you want to see me, because I've got something for you".

The doors of the car were opened.

Chris and Paul got out.

Chris spoke and laughed as if Paul was his greatest and oldest friend. And he gave Paul £200 as easily as that.

"If you don't show up, keep that. Old times' sake. No worries. Otherwise... see you tomorrow", said Chris. The heavy door to the nightclub was now open. He went inside.

Suddenly, life had taken a strange turn for the better.

Paul had some money for nothing.

And tomorrow, he was sure of it, he would be getting his hands on even more.

Paul knew what the 'something' would be. He had spent too many years now, living on the outside of life, to not know. The 'something' would either be drugs, hard drugs, to be delivered to a certain place, or a used gun to be disposed of.

Either thing was fine by Paul.

He'd be there. He'd collect.

And so he was. And so he did.

"Don't fuck this up", were the last words Chris said to him the following evening.

Chris was a major league dealer. And on the way up, he had done plenty of wrong things. But when he told Paul that there would be other work, other jobs and good money, and that he, Chris, would look after Paul, he had meant all those words. If Paul did the job, delivered the package – for it was drugs not a weapon – then Paul would be well paid. And there would always be work for someone who could be trusted.

Paul nodded. Said a few words. And went on his way with the parcel.

The thought crossed his mind that the whole place was being watched and that he was being set up to be busted. But no, there were no police lying in wait. No other gangs. Nothing. No one. Just Paul and the package.

Paul walked a few hundred metres then turned off onto the old towpath along the canal. He knew where he was supposed to go. And the canal, he had been assured, was the safest way of getting there.

As he walked along he felt the weight of the parcel.

How heavy was it? A couple of kilos at least. How much would that be worth? Very many thousands of pounds.

He stopped.

He opened the package and tasted the brown muck inside. It seemed very good.

Chris had offered Paul a great opportunity. And Paul was about to take it.

Paul turned around and went in a wholly different direction. Why should he collect a few hundred pounds when he could make thousands?

Of course a few hours later, when he found out, Chris was angry. With himself more than Paul. Why on earth had he trusted 'that fucking Peg Leg'?

He shook his head and then, looking at two square unmoving faces, he nodded. "I'm not worried about the money or the stuff", he said. "But I want him sorting out".

The two square faces nodded. And it only took a few days for them to find out where Paul was holed up; a different tower block, but still a shit hole.

Paul had achieved very little with the stolen drugs. He didn't have the sort of connections needed to sell this much stuff all at once. And for much of the last 48 hours he had sat, staring into space and drinking cheap lager.

Nevertheless, he had not lost his wits – not completely. And he was tipped off that the square faces were coming for him just a matter of minutes before they arrived.

Clearly, it was time for him to move again.

Yet another squat or bedsit.

But not here. Not in this city. No. Stealing those drugs had finished this place. Its time was over.

Paul would head for the south coast. Why not?

He had a few friends – using that word very loosely – who lived in Brighton. That was what he'd do. He would go down there. Down to Brighton.

Brighton Festival

There was a time when I knew the UK like the back of my hand. I had lived all over it. Wales, Yorkshire, Bristol, Essex and the Midlands. As kids we had taken our holidays in Scotland, Devon and the Isle of Wight. I knew the south coast from Cornwall, through to Dorset, Hampshire and Kent. Only I didn't know Sussex. Not at all. I'd never been to any part of Sussex. Not even Gatwick Airport.

But that was about to change. I no longer lived in the UK. I had homes abroad. But I was coming back for a short stay to visit a friend, and she, Joanne, now lived in Brighton.

Joanne had also spent many years in the Midlands and that was where we had first met. At art college, in Birmingham. Well, to be accurate, Joanne had been at art college, and I'd been dating another girl who attended the same place. But she was a friend of Joanne's, and so I, too, became a friend of both girls.

Joanne had then moved to London. Studying at St Martin's art school and more besides. She had worked alongside most of the 'big' names of British art. She knew people like Tracy Emin, Anish Kapoor and others. She had been in exhibitions from Sweden to Spain.

To that extent her world and mine had diverged hugely. I had more or less failed at one job after another, until, finally, a certain government agency in the UK had shown an interest in my new and rather 'unique' IT skills. That, in turn, had meant moving around a lot, especially abroad. Often spending time in hot, dusty and fairly dangerous places. But I didn't mind. It paid ridiculously well and, after 20 years or so, I was able to go completely freelance. I was now very comfortable. Set up for the rest of my life.

It was true that our worlds had diverged hugely. But we had stayed in touch on and off, over the years. At first by letter, the odd postcard, and then by emails and finally via social media.

There had been some gaps in there. We had lost touch in the 1990s for a big part of that decade, and then, more recently, we had lost touch again for a few years. Not for any particular reason, things like that just happen. It's part of life.

Just before Christmas, however, the little red icon had lit up on my Facebook page, telling me that I had a message from Joanne. And we had begun talking again, just as before, just as easily and with just as much humour.

It was then that Joanne told me she had recently moved to the south coast. To live in Brighton.

"Why?" I had asked her. "I thought you loved London and the whole scene there?"

"I do", she had replied. "But I really need a break. Some time out. Anyway, I've moved for the light, you know. After all, they call it Brighton because it is so light. Bright. You see?"

I didn't believe that. But the idea made me smile.

"Look", I said, "We must find time to actually meet up. We haven't seen each other face to face for the best part of 20 years now".

Joanne agreed.

And, although initial plans had to be cancelled for different reasons, that was why, in mid-May, I was crossing the English channel to visit Sussex, and Brighton, for the first time in my life.

I loved to travel by boat. And I always took a cabin. Even for daytime crossings.

I did use planes. Of course I did. But a boat gave me a very different feeling. Much calmer. I felt less tense. And when you have been shot at while in the air, that was understandable. That had happened twice, each time in a helicopter. Sure, catching a flight from Stansted or Manchester wasn't the same as that, but I still took a boat when the opportunity was there.

By boat, with a cabin, especially off-peak, you have peace and quiet. Space to relax and unwind. And I'd learned the hard way that such things mattered. When people lose that space – especially when they lose it for long periods of time – it damages them. Not just physical exhaustion, not even just in terms of anxiety or any obvious condition, but when people can't relax, can't unwind, they eventually lose their morale. They lose their will to go on. That is why homes are so important.

Such thoughts flashed across my mind, as they often did, as I boarded the boat but, within 15 minutes, I had taken a shower and climbed into bed.

The miles could pass and I would rest.

Sleep or not, as the boat came into the familiar waters of Portsmouth harbour, passing ships of the Royal Navy both old and new, I was ready on deck to witness our arrival.

How well I knew this place. The docks. The port. The city itself.

And the country? My country?

I'd spent so much time living and working abroad that I was no longer sure if England was still 'my' country. In truth, I asked myself that question every time I visited and every time I left.

And I had no single, settled answer. Yes, of course it was home for many reasons. But at the same time it wasn't my home. Not any longer. I'd been away for too long. Rootless, I suppose. But then what *was* home for me? I didn't really know the answer to that either.

I yawned and strolled to the other side of the boat. A distant view of the Isle of Wight. Remembering holidays taken there as a child. If I was ever to return to England, I would probably want to settle over there, on that little island. I could see the pier, at Ryde, reaching out into the Solent. I had first set foot on that pier aged about six years old and had run all the way along it, my father having to move fast to keep up with me.

But would I really want to live there now? I wasn't sure.

One of the most enlightening things about living abroad is the discovery that there is good and bad to be found everywhere. No single country is ideal. Each of them has their faults, and each of them has their strengths.

The same was true of everything.

There was no such person as the perfect person. No such thing as the ideal home. Nowhere and no thing was 'the best'. It was a question of finding what came closest. Ticked as many boxes as possible. A personal choice.

I had known Uzbeks and Pashtuns who would slit your throat to gain enough money to buy a single bullet. I had known Uzbeks and Pashtuns who would die to defend a stranger.

And there was nothing unique in that. It was the same all over.

There was a line from a film, which held true of all of us, everywhere: "I've seen knights in armour panic at the first hint of battle. And I've seen the lowliest, unarmed squire pull a spear from his own body to defend a dying horse. Nobility is not a birthright. It is defined by one's actions".

I couldn't recall the film. A kid's film, maybe? Something funny. Yet that particular line, yes, that was so true. Nobility is defined by one's actions. Bad people come in all colours, all races, all genders, all nationalities, all religions. And good people do the same. The very same. Why was that so hard to see?

I shook my head. Wrong thoughts for a few days' break.

Finally the ship had arrived.

Disembark, passports, a taxi to the station and a train for Brighton.

Joanne had told me that I would be arriving in Brighton during the middle of their festival and that, as a result, the town would be very busy with lots to see and do.

165

That sounded perfect to me. I had grown up in an artistic family and anything to do with the arts always appealed.

My father had been a painter. Not a member of the Royal Academy or anything like that, but he had produced and sold dozens of portraits in the 1940s and 1950s – before he had a family of his own. My mother, too, had been creative. She had worked in the theatre. Just like my father, her work was mainly provincial. But once or twice she had played in minor roles in London. Just like my father, once the children arrived – I was the youngest of five boys – her acting career had more or less come to an end.

My grandparents too, on my mother's side, had both been in the theatre, the difference being that they had succeeded in carrying on throughout their lives. They weren't wealthy – not even close. It was just a question of different times, different expectations, different opportunities.

Oddly one of my earliest memories was of waking up in a big wicker props basket.

I suppose, irresistibly drawn by the bright colours and soft costumes, I had crept into the basket and there found a wonderful space to imagine so many things that the imagining wore me out and I must have fallen asleep. By all accounts, if I hadn't called out at one point, I might well have woken the following day in Glasgow, because that was where my grandparents were playing next.

So, yes, for lots of reasons, I was drawn to the arts. And a festival sounded ideal.

Having stopped at every single station between Portsmouth and Brighton – which must have numbered close to 30 halts in total – my train finally arrived in the city itself.

As I got off the train, I had a brief horrible thought: would I be able to recognise Joanne after so many years? What if I walked straight past her or she did the same to me? We had aged a great deal since last seeing one another.

I needn't have worried.

Although the station concourse was every bit as busy as any London mainline station with faces and figures becoming one homogenous confusing blur, Joanne stood out. Or, to be exact, her red dress stood out. It was simply impossible to miss. My head turned when I saw it, and my slight apprehension disappeared instantly.

"Joanne", I said, turning my question into a statement as I did so.

"Helllllo!" she replied.

We reached for each other instinctively, and hugged.

"Wow", I said, "It's manic here".

"Isn't it?" Joanne replied. "Told you it would be". And then, taking my hand, she said "Come on, it's a beautiful day. Let's get out into the sun".

The front of the station was almost as chaotic as the inside, but a few steps soon took us away from the densest crowds and into the sunlight.

Joanne was right. It was a beautiful day. But, for May, it was also rather cold. An icy wind blew from the north.

"You were right to bring a big coat", said Joanne.

I was wearing an overcoat because I had been travelling since 6 am. For much of that journey, it had been unnecessary, but now, and as we walked along together, talking rapidly, towards Joanne's flat, I was very glad of it.

"I'm going back to France", I joked. "This is freezing".

"We'll be alright once we're inside", said Joanne.

Still holding hands, we soon arrived at her flat.

The flat was situated in a fine old Georgian building, at the very top, and had been divided up into a couple of bedrooms, kitchen and studio.

As soon as I saw her studio – and the view from the window – I was envious.

"What a great place", I said. "I thought you were going to have a rest from painting for a while. You won't be able to resist painting here".

Joanne laughed. "I know", she said. "I did plan to have a complete break for a few months. But... well... like you said, with a view like this and a room that makes for a perfect studio, what else could I do?"

Over a cup of tea, she showed me some of her current projects.

Still all in the preliminary stages. Sketches in pencil and charcoal, colour studies and even one or two small unfinished pieces.

And we sat, talking almost without pause, until the day's dazzling sun began to sink lower in the sky.

"Shall we go out for a drink?" Joanne asked finally. "I know a great little bar. It's part of the theatre. When there's a break in a show it fills up. But it has a really nice feel".

I remembered a theatre bar, from my days in Birmingham. A place full of characters. Bright lights, gold paintwork and decorated plaster. Actors and theatregoers. Others too. The bar in Brighton wasn't quite the same but it had a similar feel to it. Lively and happy. And it had clearly been there, as part of the theatre, for a very long time.

We sat at a table near the window and drank and had a nice evening. Some street performers enacted a play just opposite the bar – part of the festival, Joanne assured me – and drew quite a crowd. We couldn't see all of their act, from where we were sitting, but they did some incredibly athletic movements and must, surely, have been professionally trained as acrobats.

"What is it?" Joanne asked me, as I came back from the bar with our second round. "I can tell there's something".

I sat down.

Drank some of my beer.

"This place", I said. "It makes me think of my grandparents". And I told Joanne about the wicker basket.

"I didn't know", she said. "I don't think you've ever told me about your family before".

"Maybe I'm just getting old", I laughed. "But it's things like this that I miss, when I'm out of the country. You know, proper bars. Like this one. They evoke memories".

Joanne nodded.

"The last time I was in London", I continued, "It felt like all the old pubs were going. Being replaced by plate glass windows and huge balloon sized wine glasses."

"And Starbucks".

"Oh God, yes. Those things are everywhere".

"I heard a rumour", said Joanne quietly, leaning towards me, as if she was telling me a state secret, "That they are going to ban booze in bars soon. And everyone will have to sit drinking fucking Starbucks instead!"

We both laughed.

"And smoke those dreadful vapour things?"

"Yes", Joanne agreed. "Those will be compulsory".

I shook my head. "I hate the smell of those things. Sickly sweet".

And so the evening went on.

Around 11 pm, we walked back to Joanne's flat through city streets alive with police and football fans.

Manchester City had just won the title and they had done it here, in Brighton.

Millions of pounds. Players paid a fortune. We talked about it as we walked along. It all seemed crazily over the top. But the day had clearly made the Manchester fans happy, and from what we could see, they were all pretty well behaved too.

The following morning, Joanne and I were up early. That was normal for her – not for me. She had been up for at least two hours, working on some sketches, before I surfaced. But even then, for me, it was early. As she herself had once said, in terms of the hours we kept, where I was an owl, she was a lark.

"You need a nice long walk beside the sea", Joanne said, as she saw me yawning and stretching. "And perhaps a cup of tea and some cake in the park".

I glanced out of the window. It was another beautiful sunny day.

"That sounds perfect", I said. "Do you want to go now?"

Joanne shrugged. "Yes. Why not? I'm a bit stuck with this work anyway. Yes. Let's go now. We can collect a programme for the festival from the library too. Take a look and see what's on".

"OK", I said, "I'll have a shower and then get ready".

"No rush", said Joanne. She turned to her laptop, which – from what she had told me last night – was a key tool in her work these days. She often searched for images on there, as an early stage in gaining inspiration for some of her work, especially when working on a commission. She would then use the images, play around with them in Photoshop and adapt them, change them, over and over until something inside 'made sense' to her. Initially I'd said that it sounded a bit like cheating. But Joanne was adamant that it was no different to what artists had always done;

even greats like Vermeer had used the latest gadget – a camera obscura. So, yes, why not use a laptop? It made sense.

I came back from my shower, feeling a lot brighter, and more or less dressed ready to go.

"I've been checking out the programme of events for the festival", said Joanne, looking up from her computer screen. "And there are quite a few things that sound interesting. We should definitely go to one or two of them".

I nodded and sat down.

"Listen to this one", she continued. "It's an installation". And she read direct from the monitor. "Twisted Patterns. Twisted Patterns is a free exhibition using sound, projections and dance to immerse the audience in the imaginary landscape of the artist's mind. The work is inspired by the artists own neurological disorder which causes visual distortions such as flickering and the appearance of auras. The audience will experience a mythical version of how the artist sees the world, entering an alternate AsianSpace (an Asian perspective on the politics and our culture of technology) reality, inspired by research into the neuroscience of perception and drawing on rituals of Hindu origin".

To be honest, most of that had washed over me without very much of it registering. I had been to countless exhibitions across much of Europe, but I was still firmly attached to canvases and oil

paint. Dance, too, I enjoyed. Music, of course. But installations –
art installations – had never really done anything for me.

All the same, I was always ready to take a look at something new.
Who knows? It had taken me many years before I could
understand and appreciate the Cubism of Picasso and Braque.
Perhaps the same would be true of installations.

"Shall we go to that?" Joanne asked, once again looking up at me.

I nodded. "Yeah. Yes. The mixture of neurological science and
artistic expression sounds interesting. What else is there?"

Joanne passed me her laptop, a small white thing, hardly any
larger than an iPad and said, "Have a look online, while I nip to
the loo and get ready".

I took the laptop, pausing to glance out of the window as a seagull
landed on the gutter and shouted its wildly cheerful call. The bird
saw me move, took fright and flew off. I smiled. It would be great
to walk along by the sea again.

I read the festival programme. Artists from Ghana and Mali,
Egypt and Syria. I read about the Malian singer and songwriter.
She was a beautiful woman. But what was her music like? I found
a link on YouTube to some of her work. Listened to that. It was
wonderful. I had once been to Mali and travelled on the Niger
River. Her songs took me back there.

Then, suddenly, and for no apparent reason, I had a feeling of not being represented. Simply that. As if I didn't count.

Ghana and Mali.

Egypt and Syria.

I had grown up on a fairly poor white estate in the Midlands. What was there at the festival that spoke to me? What spoke for me?

I skimmed through a few more of the links. The artists, the artistes, were clever, creative and often brilliant. But where were the poor white English males? There were none and I felt excluded.

Joanne came back in. "You OK? Ready to go?"

I shrugged. Whatever my thoughts had been about the festival, it didn't matter. "Yes", I said. "Nothing serious. Come on. The seaside first. A long walk".

A long walk was exactly what we took.

All the way along the front, in the sun, still with that bitter wind, out to and well past Kemptown. Then we turned, and walked all the way back. Past the main pier until we found ourselves beneath a brand new tower on the sea front.

"It's got a revolving restaurant, or something", said Joanne, as we both craned our necks to look up at the thing. "It goes up and down. Slowly. But all the same, it doesn't sound like it would be great for the digestion. Up and down, up and down".

"Revolving or revolting?"

"Probably both", said Joanne looking up at the tower.

I laughed and climbed into a giant deckchair situated at the base of the tower.

"I shan't tell you what the local nickname for the tower is", Joanne added, clambering up into the deckchair and sitting next to me.

"Why not?" I asked.

"It's rude!" she laughed.

We sat for a while in that oversized chair, watching the world go by. Talking about this and that. Nothing in particular.

"This is fantastic", said Joanne, meaning the chair. "I had no idea you could sit in it".

I looked at her and frowned. "You mean you've walked past this thing before and never climbed up and sat in it?"

Joanne shook her head.

I laughed. "It is brilliant", I agreed. "If I was homeless, this is where I would aim for every night".

A crowd of people walked past wearing silver tin foil hats, blowing horns and dressed in the most colourful clothes. Protesting about something – but we weren't sure what – and having fun too.

"Brighton's a nice place", I said. "The people here seem to be mostly quite happy".

Joanne nodded.

And for a short while longer, we sat, legs dangling.

"Listen", said Joanne, "There's a gallery just near here, a private gallery, and the owner is thinking of putting on some of my work. Let's go and take a look at the place".

"OK", I said. "But then I want that tea in the park you promised me".

From the giant deckchair we walked a little further out of town, and then along a side street. This end of the city appeared to me to be more affluent and I said as much to Joanne.

She agreed. We were coming towards Hove now, she explained.

"And that", she concluded, making a 'moneyed' gesture with her fingers, "Is why there are private art galleries up here".

We found the gallery, a handsome building which must, once, have been an old garage. Perhaps back in the 1930s, when rich people drove cars like Bentleys and everyone else walked.

The gallery wasn't large. But it was a nice space and it had the right sort of feel to it.

"Good choice", I whispered to Joanne, as we looked at some of the work currently being displayed.

"The painting?" Joanne said, raising an eyebrow at the piece we stood in front of.

"No", I said, "No. I meant this gallery. Good choice of gallery for your show. That painting is awful".

And so it was. It was a small but stylish gallery, but the stuff on display, on that particular day, was mostly pretty poor. As if a charity shop had amassed a lot of unwanted amateur work from the 1970s, and then decided to put it all on show.

"Oh my Lord", I whispered again, as I saw the price on one of the pieces.

Both Joanne and I came to the conclusion that the artist must be related to the gallery owner. And that both, to judge by the prices being asked, had a rather unrealistic idea of the value of money or this particular artist.

Of course inside the gallery itself, we made polite noises about what we'd seen. But once outside and having walked well out of sight, we couldn't help but laugh out loud.

"Oh my God", said Joanne. "Most of that stuff was terrible! £1500 for someone who hasn't even learned how to draw."

"£1500 and a lot more". I said. "Some of them cost much more than that. But will any of it sell for those kinds of prices?"

Joanne nodded and feigned a very posh southern voice. "In Hove, oh yes darling. In fact, really, you've no idea how much money some people have and are very happy to spend. I sold a piece through a gallery for £6,000 last year. And it was only a sketch, really".

I stopped. "Is that true? £6,000 for a drawing?" I repeated the figure.

Joanne nodded and smiled. "Afraid so".

"I'm in the wrong business".

"Well, yes. But that was a gallery in Chelsea", said Joanne. "They throw money around up there like there's no tomorrow, even more than they do here".

From the gallery, we walked to the park. It wasn't far, and the roads were quiet, clean and tidy. Suburbia was alive and well and still available to middle England.

I told myself that I liked it. And I did like it. Brighton felt a happy place.

We sat in the park for about an hour and a half. We took tea and cake, then more tea and finally a toasted sandwich. And as we sat there, sheltered from the remorselessly chilly wind and with the sun beating down, all the troubles of the world felt a million miles away.

Children played on the slides and swings, whilst mothers – it was mainly mothers – looked on. Some women were talking to friends, some were alone and reading, and a few others came through the park jogging. One or two groups of people, like us, relaxed in front of the little cafe, drinking tea or coffee, chatting with friends and enjoying the day.

I had always loved municipal parks, ever since my childhood. And this one took me right back to those carefree days.

"I don't know what time the exhibition starts", said Joanne suddenly.

"No", I said. "Nor do I. Will it be on this afternoon, do you think?"

Joanne shrugged. "This evening probably. But we should go and check".

"Back to yours?"

"No, we'll go into town and I'll show you the library. It's one of my favourite places; I spend hours there on some days. And we can check the times of festival events in there too".

Brighton library was a 15-minute walk from the park, and turned out to be a non-descript glass block, nestled in a street wholly lacking in character. Parts of Brighton still had warmth, but here, for some reason, everything had been rebuilt recently in a particularly soulless manner.

As we approached the library from the direction of the coast – not for the first time Joanne had got us a little lost – we had to cross a small featureless square. The kind of paved space that might accommodate a 'farmers' market two mornings a week in an attempt to provide the area with some charm.

"Oh", said Joanne. "What are those?"

In the middle of the square, a woman appeared to be doing some kind of street performance or, rather, street art. Part of the festival? It was impossible to tell.

"What are they?" asked Joanne, as we got closer.

"I'm not sure", I replied, stopping to look at the work. "Ask her".

The art appeared to be around 15 or so ordinary white pillows with faces painted on them. Just ordinary pillows. A little bit shabby, perhaps, from lying in the street and being painted, but other than that, nothing particularly exceptional.

"Excuse me", said Joanne to the woman. "Did you paint these?"

The woman, who was evidently packing up for the day, stopped and looked up. Then she stood up, and smiled. A broad but sad sort of smile. "Yes", she replied.

I was taken aback by the woman's appearance. She was polite and bright eyed, but she also had the look of someone who had fallen on hard times. Her clothes were tired, her face too. Something in her world was clearly wrong, or perhaps it was something she had experienced, and whatever it was, it was now fatiguing her soul. I had seen that look before, many times, in countries torn apart by war.

"What are they?" Joanne asked the artist, her question interrupting my thoughts.

I glanced down once more at the pillows, at the painted faces, and noticed that each of them had a name. Each face had a name painted next to it.

"They are the faces of people who have died, here in Brighton, during the last 12 months", said the painter.

For a moment neither Joanne nor I knew what to say.

"Died?" I finally asked.

"Homeless", said the woman, flatly. "They were all homeless here in the city. And they died".

"Oh my God", said Joanne.

I looked down at the pillow nearest to me. And read the name aloud. "Akeem", I said.

Joanne read the next name. "Nicola".

I looked at the others.

"Wasim".

"Lori".

"Paul".

Joanne stood next to me. And we looked at the faces for a while.

Wondered who they were. Wondered how they had ended up living on the streets. Homeless.

Homeless and dying in Brighton.

Afterword

by Lindsay Jones

on behalf of

Thank you to Geoff for choosing to support the work of Shelter and including us in the journey of this book.

Dying in Brighton tells an interesting and compelling story, bringing the real human aspect to the issues and problems facing far too many people who are homeless, facing homelessness or living in poor or temporary accommodation in Britain today.

Shelter was founded in 1966 by a group who came together after being appalled by the state and lack of availability of decent housing for people in the UK at that time. They lobbied parliament for change and set about advising people as to how to improve their situation. Despite tireless work and many changes to law, sadly we are needed more than ever today to help people who are homeless, facing homelessness or bad housing.

We campaign, support, advocate, represent and help people to remain in their home, find a home or fight for a home. We campaign to bring about system change and fight for what is right and will not stop until everyone is in a safe, home.

We are a charity and every penny raised helps us to help more people. By buying this book you are helping us to hep people like the characters within it. Thank you so much.

To find our more about our work, how to access our services or how to support us visit www.shelter.org.uk or email lindsay_jones@shelter.org.uk

More stuff!

Reviews

If you got this far, THANK YOU! I hope you enjoyed the book. Please take a moment to click on this link and give it a review.

https://www.amazon.co.uk/dp/B081854HBJ

Another book, by the same author, which might be of interest

"The girl sitting opposite me wasn't a girl, she was a boy!"
Blond(e) BOY, Red LIPSTICK
An old fashioned romance... but with a difference.
Available on Amazon:
https://www.amazon.co.uk/dp/B07L7XPWKP
"A real page turner, it made me laugh and cry often at the same time"

Contact

For more information, any questions or just to say "Hello", please feel free to get in touch at info@geoffbunn.com

Printed in Great Britain
by Amazon

22123361R00108